PROJECT MEGALODON

ALEX LAYBOURNE

SEVERED PRESS
HOBART TASMANIA

PROJECT MEGALODON

Copyright © 2016 Alex Laybourne
Copyright © 2016 by Severed Press

WWW.SEVEREDPRESS.COM

ISBN: 978-1-925493-20-7

This is for my wife Patty, and our children, James, Logan, Ashleigh, Damon and Riley.

CHAPTER 1

Dr. Martin Lucas sauntered through his lab without a care in the world. He moved with the air of a man who had everything. So he did. He worked for the U.S. government on a fully functional laboratory on a deep-sea-stationed platform. Having been recruited by the military at a young age, he spent many years working in dodgy countries on all manner of secret projects. A succession of jobs which varied from being as dull as dishwater to something a little less exciting than watching paint dry.

Until one day, the call came in. His skillset recommended him as being one of several potential candidates for a biological study on the high-tech Omega-Base-Six. The station was well known through the military. Having cost an arm and a leg to construct, and running almost a full year behind schedule, the chance to work on the base was something anybody with a knowledge of the military would have jumped at.

Being a single man, with no dependents, not even a set of ageing parents or annoying siblings to come looking for him, Martin's name quickly rose to the top pile.

His interview went without a hitch. His performance was one even he was happy with as he walked out of the room. The chief dark-suited stranger even laughed at one point. The good kind of laugh, not the pity-filled expression that comprised most of Martin's high school years.

In the two intervening years since the interview, only two things eluded Martin's own personal investigation. Who the hell they were, and how they got the job doing … whatever they did. It certainly wasn't recorded anywhere. Hell, he wagered that even the aliases of their aliases were too deeply buried to be found.

So Martin relocated onto Omega-Base-Six and collected a handsome salary every month. With no real way to spend it beyond the minimum amount he needed for sundries and snacks, he amassed a small fortune. It was not wasted money, every cent played a role in his future. A nice retirement home in a warm climate. A set of state-of-the-art Calloway clubs and a trophy wife he could either trade in every few years or at least have upgraded surgically whenever she needed it.

Three scientists worked on the platform. Each received their own station on the large hexagonal structure. Martin knew them all by name, but their association ended at that. The competition among them was fierce. Each claimed their own specialty and never hesitated to demonstrate to those that mattered just how good they were.

Martin's passion was biological. He had worked at the CDC for several years, early in his career, but that had not been enough. Diseases were powerful, but they were too small. Martin wanted his work to be visible. So he had entered the military and worked on bio-technology for injured soldiers. Limbs and appendages that went above and beyond the standard smooth-moving plastic joints. Then he moved onto fully active biological suits.

Protective clothing that was alive and worked together with the wearer to form a second skin that could cope with the more hostile environments that soldiers were often required to work within.

At first, the project was regarded as nothing more than a side show. Some experimental department. But then the bombs had dropped. Chemical and biological weapons that had changed the tide of war and given the terrorists an iron grip over the Middle East and almost all of Africa. All of a sudden the need for bio-technology was not just on the up, but rather, it was the first word on everybody's lips. The military needed a new level of security, both home and abroad.

This, of course, included the civilian branch. That was where the real money was made, and with the cost of war increasing, the US government ensured that all licensed biological protection products were manufactured through their own industries.

Martin enjoyed working in the civilian sector. It had made a welcome break from the deserts and mountains. The paycheck was less, but he got to live a quiet life, with enough left over each month to start laying the foundations for his future, but deep down, Martin missed the thrill of the front line, or what served as the front line for a lab rat.

When the call came, and the men in suits summoned him, Martin jumped at the prospect of returning to the active side of military weapons technology.

Now, standing in his lab on Omega-Base-Six, Tim McGraw blasting through his headphones, Martin was waiting for the delivery of something very special. When they signed their contracts, each of the scientists on board, received the same simple instruction. A reminder for them all for when the time came to make difficult decisions. They were working on weapons. Implements of destruction the purpose of which being help swing the tide of war back in the allies favour.

For the majority of his time since arriving, Martin's work had been theoretical. The plans he drew up were not the ones you just dove into head first. Unless of course the plan involved blowing yourself up or eaten, depending on the nature of the project you botched.

The hands fell on Martin's shoulders just as Tim started jamming about his stained white T-shirt. Martin jumped and spun around. He pulled the headphones off and fumbled for the button to silence the machine.

That done, he quickly stood straight, his spine rigid, and stared at the two Marines who had disturbed him.

"Sorry to disturb you, Doctor," one of the two thick-jawed, stony-eyed men spoke. "We need you to come with us."

"What is this about?" Martin asked, not concerned but intrigued.

"I cannot say, sir. All I know is there is a package for you, and that you need to come with us and collect it yourself," the second Marine answered. He looked identical to his colleague, the spitting image.

"Okay, let me just put these things—" Martin moved towards his plans and documents that he would never leave out in plain sight when he was not around.

"Now, sir. I am afraid this matter cannot wait," Marine number one spoke.

"Fine, fine I'm coming," Martin said with a sigh. He gathered his papers and threw them into one of the drawers of the desk against the rear wall of the lab. Much to the disapproval of the waiting Marines.

The compound was a three-tiered structure, with the lower level resting beneath the ocean's surface. The hexagonal structure was secured by a circular pillar beneath each corner. The pillars also served as the emergency escape routes, with a submarine dock attached to three of the six leg turrets. Elevator shafts ran through the center of each, along with an emergency ladder that ran along the inside of the exterior wall. The main body of the base was designed to float in the event of a catastrophic occurrence. It was even rumoured that it could be manually detached and steered like any other water craft. But that was more talk among the grunts that formed the bulk of the staff on site.

While they were only three in number, science was the main focal point of Omega-Base-Six. That was why Martin walked with such confidence as he was marched through the halls. All eyes were turned to the slightly chubby scientist with his unkempt hair and piss-poor attempt at facial hair, but none of that bothered him, because Martin understood that beneath it all, he was the reason the base existed, well, one of the reasons. He also knew, from brief conversations with a young Marine not long after he arrived, that everybody on board had been placed on a salary substantially more than others of their rank stationed elsewhere.

"So, you guys just came to invite me to dinner, is that it?" Martin asked as they led him towards the dining area.

Neither of the Marines spoke.

"Not big talkers, huh?" Martin looked from one man to the other.

Both men stopped walking so abruptly that Martin didn't have time to react, and he was pulled back sharply when their grip on his arms stopped his momentum.

"Woah, guys, I was just kidding around. Take it easy," he said, more than a few nerves bouncing in his voice. Thinking you had control over things, and actually putting your money where your mouth was, were two very different things to Martin.

"In here," one of the square-jawed brothers spoke.

"Here?"

"Yes, here," the second brother answered, pressing a button that made the wall disappear revealing a hidden elevator. Blue lightning ran along the edges. The walls, floor, and roof of the elevator were made of steel, polished to a reflective shine. As they moved inside and the doors closed, it felt, and looked, as if Martin was standing there with twenty other people.

"So, where are we going?" Martin tried again. He was starting to feel nervous, and when that happened, his chatty side came to the surface.

"To your new lab," one answered.

"Shut up," the other growled, punching his twin in the ribs.

"Sorry, but, well, it's kind of obvious now, right?"

"I guess, but ah fuck it. You are heading to your new lab. There are some people who are very interested in talking to you," Brother number two offered. "Are you happy now?" he addressed his brother.

"Ecstatic, thank you."

Before their brotherly quarrel could develop any further, the elevator announced their arrival with a distinctive ping, and the doors slid open.

The two Marines left the lift, leaving Martin standing alone, staring into some sort of secret lab. By the time they realized he had not followed them, the doors had closed and the elevator had risen back to the top of the shaft.

It took several minutes of fumbling before Martin found the buttons, which were nothing but sensors built into the wall, and brought himself back down.

When the doors opened this time, he was sure to move before they fully retracted.

"Sorry about that, but this place is mind blowing," he said in a distracted voice, as his eyes continued to search the room, somehow missing the four unamused faces that were standing over from him.

"Nice of you to join us, Dr. Lucas," one of the men spoke.

Martin had no idea who he was, but he was dressed in a black suit, with a white shirt, black tie and slicked back black hair. He looked every inch the secret, no-name agency operative.

"Yeah, sorry about that, the lift, it kind of … yeah." Martin fell quiet when the general pushed to the front of the group. "Sorry, sir."

"Dr. Lucas, this is not some high school science camp. I did not pick you for this project because of your charms, but because of your brilliance. I hope we will not have more incidents like this." General Burke cut an imposing figure and was widely known as a man not to be messed with.

"No, sir, sorry, sir," Martin fired his answer, standing to attention as he did.

"Good, then let's get this moving. We have no time to waste. We have acquired a rather unique specimen, and it has been the decision of people above even my pay grade to gift it to you, Dr. Lucas. Both it, and this laboratory are now yours."

"Mine," Martin interrupted, regretting it immediately.

"For now, yes, but interrupt me again and you will be fed to this creature instead of raising it. Are we clear?"

Martin said nothing.

"That was a question. Now you can speak," the general snarled.

"Sorry, sir. Yes, I understand. But this … this lab. I don't fully understand," Martin stuttered.

"Allow me to interrupt, General Burke," the suited man spoke as he took a step forward. "Dr. Lucas. I have been a fan of your work for some time. I am sure you understand that Omega-Base-Six is somewhat of a special facility. We are not here in the name peace, Dr. Lucas. The time for such mistruths has long since passed us by. We are a station of war. What we have discovered is a creature of legend. It alone would be a formidable weapon, could we but harness its natural tendencies. What we want, Dr. Lucas, is for you to nurture this creature, to raise it, and to turn it into the ultimate weapon. The war in the east is far from over, and the sea is going to play a key role for both sides. Do you understand what I am saying?"

"Yes." Martin nodded. "I understand, but what exactly have you found?"

"I am glad you ask, but first, I think it is time for a few people to leave us now." The man threw a single glance to the two Marines. Further words were not needed for the order to be understood. Both men offered a salute, turned and marched into the elevator. "That includes you, General," the man in the suit spoke.

"I beg your—" The general was aghast at the mere notion of being made to leave.

"You will do well to remember who you are talking to," the man in the suit barked.

"Sir," the general offered with enough respect to keep the man quiet, but the right level of attitude to make Martin smile.

The lift doors opened and the general moved inside. He did not turn around to face them men he left behind, but his gaze was reflected on the polished walls.

"He didn't look very happy," Martin said as the lift could be heard rising once more.

"I don't really care. You are the reason I am here, not some general with a power problem," the suited man spoke.

"Okay, but, who are you?" Martin asked. He faced the man, and could not help but allow his eyes to wander around the lab he had just been gifted.

"Of course. My name is Agent Callaghan, more than that you do not need to know. Who I work for exactly is irrelevant, because the top of the chain is the US government, the same as you. Dr. Lucas, I know you are no stranger to war. You know of its impact and the resulting condition the Middle East has found itself in. We want to put a stop to this reign of terror. We are building up the war effort, and as I said, naval warfare will play a large role. Sorry, I am repeating myself." Agent Callaghan caught his second explanation and smiled. "Maybe it is better if I showed you the rest."

"The rest," Martin gasped.

"Yes," Callaghan spoke without emotion. "This is the upper level of the lab, but beneath your feet, well, let's take a look. It is waiting for you."

"It?"

Agent Callaghan said nothing further, but pressed a button on the wall and the floor began to vibrate. "You might want to take a large step to your right," he said just as the floor began to shift.

The large panel slid away revealing a staircase to a second level.

"Wow, a hidden room inside the hidden room. You guys, don't mess around, do you?" Martin joked.

"No, we don't," Callaghan answered with a straight face. "After you."

Martin made his way down the stairs, the lighting coming on as he moved. The second floor of the lab was a little smaller than the first, but filled will all manner of equipment, from microscopes to scanners, centrifuges and incubators.

"Wow, this is a third degree C1-Si laser scanning confocal microscope." Martin ran his hands over the machine. "I've got the second degree upstairs—"

"Actually, this is a fourth-degree model. The only one of its kind," Callaghan interrupted.

"Fourth degree, you know what the means?" Martin asked excitedly.

"No."

"Oh, never mind then." Martin could not keep his eyes still long enough to truly take it all in.

He saw two hybridization ovens, and PCR machines, a cluster of electrophoresis chambers and molecular gels, not to mention the nutators, orbital shakers and blot machines. Computers were split over both floors, and Martin knew from looking that each one had a specific purpose. No more juggling seven systems on three screens from a centrally housed server. It took a while before Martin even saw the large glass tank that occupied the center of the lab.

"We found it by chance," Callaghan spoke once he saw Martin's eyes fall on the tank. "As is often the case, the best discoveries are made when you are looking for something else."

The circular tank was enormous, easily large enough to hold the largest of all creatures, a blue whale. The hidden lab, must have stretched the entire expanse of the base, with the lower level deeper, but not as wide.

"What is in the tank?" Martin moved closer.

"Your new baby. Take a look." Callaghan leaned over and tapped the glass three times.

For a moment, there was nothing.

"Wait for it," Callaghan said calmly.

Martin did not say anything. He could make out the blurred shape in the water. The creature drew closer. The shark was the size of a large dog, with a tall dorsal fin and a strange-looking mouth, which seemed to extend further along the body than any shark Martin had ever seen, and the nose had a slight upwards turn which only served to make the creature look even more vicious.

"A shark, you want me to weaponize a shark?" Martin asked with wide-eyed and slack-jawed fascination. He was like a kid at Christmas, coming down to find a mountain of gifts all with his name on them.

Agent Callaghan looked at Martin and smiled. "I knew we had made the right choice," he spoke, nodding his head. "Very good, Dr. Lucas. Only, that is no ordinary shark."

"It doesn't look like one," Martin answered. "What sort of cross breed is it? I will need to know what I am working with."

"This is no crossbreed. It is a Megalodon, as purebred as you could hope for."

"A Megalodon?" Martin coughed. "They don't exist." He spoke to Agent Callaghan, but could not pull his eyes from the tank.

"That is what we thought also. Like I said, we stopped looking, and there it was," Callaghan said as he moved beside Martin. "Isn't it something? A baby, a blank slate at the top of the food chain. Your blank slate, Doctor. I hope you will not disappoint us."

Martin heard the words, but was lost at the sight of the shark. The creature was floating in the tank and seemed to be staring at him. It swam back and forth, but never to the point where eye contact with Martin was broken.

"I can let myself out. Remember, Dr. Lucas, we expect something extraordinary to come from this. If you disappoint us, the repercussions will be severe." With that, Agent Callaghan turned and left.

He was in the elevator and heading up to the main section of the base before Martin looked up to respond to the threat that had been whispered to him.

CHAPTER 2

"Yes, sir, I took him down there myself," Ronny Huyberts spoke into the burner cell that his brother had managed to arrange. "Should we make a move?"

"Not yet. Let him work. We want to know what he is working on. Keep an eye on him. Report back when you know more," a gravelly voice spoke on the other end of the phone.

"Yes, sir. You can count on me," Ronny answered.

"Us, he can count on us," Philip, his twin brother whispered. Ronny shushed him with a flap of his hand, but Phillip glared at him, making it clear he was not done with his protestations.

"Mr. Huyberts, you will need to destroy this phone. We will organize another for you when the time is right."

The line went dead before Ronny had the chance to answer. A few moments later, the phone died completely.

"What did they say?" Philip asked.

"Nothing. We have to wait. Keep an eye on the good doctor." Ronny looked at his brother and smiled. "Cheer up, brother, we are on the way now. No turning back."

"No turning back," Philip repeated, his voice sounding less than confident.

Ronny laughed and clapped his brother on the shoulder. He folded the phone over on itself, snapping the unit in two before throwing it through the open window in the hall. A few moments later, they were in line in the canteen, waiting for food. By the time they were sitting at their usual table, both men had received a note, slid to them by an unknown, and always unseen, ally.

They ate in silence, until they were joined by the others in their group. Jones, Wilson, McCoy and Dudek. The six of them ate every meal together and shared a bunking station. They had arrived on Omega-Base-Six together, and while none knew each other beforehand, they grew closer than brothers.

"What were you guys doing with the scientist?" McCoy asked as they ate.

Ronny looked at Philip, waiting to see if he would answer. When he didn't, Ronny took the lead. "Oh, we had to take him to a meeting. Order from the general himself."

"What was it all about?" Dudek asked.

"No idea, we just delivered him and got the hell out of there," Ronny answered.

"Yes, we didn't want to stay and watch," Philip added.

"So what do you think it was?" Dudek pushed.

"Yeah, I mean we all know something is going on around this base. Something bigger than they are telling us," Jensen Jones spoke with a mouthful of chow.

"Damned if I know. Maybe they are axing him," Philip offered.

"Unlikely. No, there is something going on there. Where did you take him?" Wilson interrupted the conversation.

Ronny looked at Philip, and Philip looked at Ronny.

"Um, we just took him to the main deck. You know there's all kinds of meeting rooms up there." Ronny breathed a sigh of relief for his brother's quick thinking.

One Month Later.

Martin didn't hear the doors to the elevator open. He was lost in his work, on the second level. The floor was sealed, nobody would be able to find him if they didn't know the layout of the lab.

In the tank before him, the Megalodon had tripled in size already, and its nose had lengthened considerably, making room for the multiple rows of serrated teeth that lined its mouth.

Martin had his eyes glued to a microscope. He added a drop of a solution onto the petri-dish he was examining and watched, holding his breath.

"Hell yeah!" he roared, slapping his hands together.

"Good news, Dr. Lucas," the voice spoke from nowhere, causing Martin to jump and stumble backwards into the workstation. Several empty glass beakers fell to the floor and shattered.

In the tank, the Megalodon sensed the disruption and grew restless in an instant. It swam back and forth in the tank, the waters churning.

Agent Callaghan stepped down into the lab, taking his time. He looked at the devastation. The shards of broken glass and the general odour of hard work. A staleness that spoke of long hours, infrequent showers and the kind of sweat that came from a mixture of stress and exertion.

"I hope I did not startle you," Callaghan said with a smile.

"No, um … well, a little. I've not had any company down here for, well, I'm not sure how long," Martin spoke, trying to hide the fact that his heart was racing in his chest.

"I had heard your appearances out of the lab had all but dried up." The smile fell from Callaghan's face and a look of concern replaced it. "I know there is pressure on this project, Dr. Lucas, but I am well aware of the dangers overworking a person can bring. You should not dedicate every moment to this place. You need to rest, to head outside and take in a sunrise, or something. You will do me no good fried, or worn out."

Martin was not sure if the man was being genuine, or if he was only thinking about the long-term success of the project.

"It's fine, really. I am not much of a social person, and I do go outside. I head up top at night. I like to look at the stars." Martin spoke as if they were old friends.

"Very good." Callaghan smiled again. "Now, how is my super weapon coming along?" He turned his attention to the tank. The Megalodon had sunk back into the tank. He reached up and tapped three times on the glass.

"I wouldn't do that if I were you, Agent," Martin spoke hurried. He moved to stand beside the agent and stared at the tank.

"Why not?"

"Because she only listens to me." Martin was no fool.

"To you?" There was a tone of surprise to Callaghan's voice.

"For now, yes. She is in training. When I am done, she will be yours to command." Martin felt compelled to explain himself.

"Very good, Dr. Lucas. Out of curiosity, how do you know the creature is a female?"

"It is a killing machine, Agent. Cold and ruthless. How could that not be a woman?" Martin looked at Callaghan and gave him a smile.

Callaghan stood for a moment, taken aback by the doctor's words. He then smiled, and laughed. "I have two ex-wives that certainly prove your theory correct."

Both men laughed.

"What can I do for you, Agent? Surely you are not expecting results already?" Martin asked light-heartedly. "You can't be serious," he added when he caught the stony expression on Callaghan's face.

"I told you at the start that this project was important. There are a lot of interested parties waiting for this weapon. I am expecting to see some results, yes," Callaghan answered.

"Progress, I can give you progress, but results … That would mean you expect the finished article, and Agent Callaghan, she's still a baby." Martin turned to face the tank. The Megalodon appeared, emerging from the murky water as if materializing from nothing.

"I will not argue semantics with you, Dr. Lucas. Not even I, nor my superiors, would expect the finished product just yet. We will require some field testing, I am sure you can understand that. For now, however, a report from you and your continued dedication to the cause is all that I ask."

The shark hovered in the tank, swimming back and forth like a tiger in the zoo. It was agitated, ready to fight, to hunt … to kill.

"I have been studying its DNA, and slowly integrating some of the bio-technology we have used in previous weapons, to ensure its bite becomes venomous. This is a side project to my real research. After all, you want this creature for a naval weapon, and there won't be much for it to poison out in the deep water." Martin spoke quickly, not wanting to give Callaghan the time to question him. "I have also worked on engineering not only a thickened, hardened skin, but also the teeth. Sharks are known to, shall we say, cycle through their teeth. I have made it so that the teeth are sturdier and less prone to being lost. Already a third row of teeth has sprouted through the gums of this beauty."

"How do you plan on controlling her?" Agent Callaghan took everything on board, accepting it without question.

Martin paused. He was split between two options, both of which would require different approaches. "I was thinking of a microchip inserted into the brainstem. We could then access it with a computer and effectively guide her anywhere we wanted. It's a dangerous procedure, and with only one of these magnificent creatures to play with, I am sceptical." Martin paused, waiting for Callaghan to say something.

"Don't be, Dr. Lucas. I have full faith in your work, as for my superiors, well, I am sure you will not disappoint them. I have enough information for now and will leave you to your studies. Remember, try taking a break every now and then."

"Thank you, sir... Agent ... um ... right, I'd better get back to it." Martin smiled and turned away, knowing Callaghan could find his own way out.

***

"Johnson, Johnson, do you copy?" Jeffrey Callaghan spoke into his radio as he rode up in the lift.

"Yes, sir. Loud and clear," Randy Johnson answered. He sat behind the controls of the Bell helicopter on the landing pad located on the upper-most platform Omega-Base-Six had to offer.

The sea stretched in all directions, an endless, undulating mass of gun-steel grey. It wasn't helped by the overcast sky and the threat of rain which hung heavy in the air around them.

"I've finished with the good doctor. I am making my way back up now. Please prepare for departure. I'd like to be on dry land before the storm hits." Callaghan was not a fan of helicopter travel. He had survived two crashes in his life, but both were in fixed wing aircraft. He had known plenty of men to be involved in helicopter crashes. He had read eulogies at their funerals.

"Yes, sir. I will have us ready for the off in five minutes," Johnson answered. A fifteen-year veteran of the Marine Corps, Randy Johnson was one of the best pilots in the game, and a man who had worked closely with Callaghan for several years, after his heroics in an Iraqi rescue mission earned him a special placement away from the active front.

"Perfect. I have one more stop to make, but I don't expect any delays," Callaghan offered, before shutting down his radio as the elevator he was riding reached the top. The wall opened, and Callahan slipped unseen into the working level of the base.

Callaghan moved through the crowd like a ghost. Nobody noticed him, nobody would remember seeing him. That was just how things went. It was nothing supernatural, nothing out of this world. It was a simple fact that Agent Jeffrey Callaghan could move through places unseen. He blended in. It was all part of the training, part of the job. Being better than the best of the best. He was not the only one, far from it, but he was good at what he did.

Callaghan knew where the brothers would be. He moved to the upper level, where there was a series of open-air sections that allowed the officers stationed on Omega-Base-Six the fresh air and exercise they needed.

Ronny and Philip were not at either of the basketball courts, nor were they in the large, state-of-the-art gym, where an array of equipment and free weights lay heavily used by some and unheard of by others.

The Huyberts brothers were in the smokers' area. They were on their own, which only made Callaghan's final job that much easier. He pulled out his service weapon, a SIG Sauer P226, and screwed the silencer in place.

Callaghan knew his targets and felt no need to let them know their demise was coming. He raised his pistol and fired twice. Blood misted the air, caught in the wind that was always present this far out at sea. The bodies fell to the floor. Ronny had a neat hole placed in the center of his forehead, while Philip was taken by a shot through the temple.

Neither stood a chance.

Callaghan moved fast, and without thinking, lifted up each body and threw them overboard. They crashed into the ocean and would either be eaten by the sharks or crushed by the tide against the legs of the structure. Either way, he didn't care. He had a job to do, and a brand new bank balance waiting for him when he got back to shore.

"We are all ready and cleared to depart," Randy's voice came through the headset.

"I am now on my way," Callaghan answered as he disassembled his weapon and slid it back into the inside of his jacket.

Callaghan walked towards the chopper with a smile on his face. The initial guilt he had experienced when first given the chance to betray his country had been significant. He had not slept well for several weeks leading up to the opportunity, but now that the deed was done, he felt as if a weight had been lifted from his shoulders.

Three paces later, his head was lifted from his shoulders as the rifle round cut through his throat, severing his spine in the process. Agent Callaghan fell to the floor of the helipad a few moments later.

Randy Johnson didn't like discharging his weapon, but when needs must, he would do it. It was all part of the training, part of the job. Being better than the best of the best. He was not the only one, far from it, but he was good at what he did.

Randy lifted the body of the man he would have given his life for, until six months earlier, and deposited it in the back of the helicopter. He was under strict orders to return the body, and Randy understood it was never recommended to ask questions of his superiors.

CHAPTER 3

The storm set in at the start of the day. Before first light, the waves were as tall as the platform, and the gusts of wind that hit were strong enough to shake the building and have everybody on edge. Marines or not, the idea of being stuck in the middle of what was rapidly being labelled a superstorm was not something they had signed on for.

Lightning lit up the sky, while the rising sun was hidden by a sky so heavy with storm it made time of day indeterminable.

"It's damned rough out there," Dudek said as they stood in one of the outer corridors, watching the sea grow wilder with each passing minute.

"Never seen anything as crazy as this, and I spent my whole live out on the ocean," Wilson said with admiration in his voice. "You got to always respect the sea, man."

"I heard they are calling it a superstorm, or some shit like that," McCoy tried to laugh the situation off, but all he did was capture the nervousness that had fallen over the entire facility.

The wind gusted, and a wall of water hit the windows where they stood. The glass was double-reinforced, military grade, but the force of the assault could not be hidden. It made the men fall quiet and got them moving.

"Ronny would have gotten a kick out of this," Jones said as they sat down in the mess hall.

"Yeah, God rest his soul," Wilson added, making the sign of the cross as he did.

"I still can't believe it. I mean, both of them, an accident like that. How can something like that happen?" Jones spoke.

"Makes you wonder," Dudek began.

"Dude, please, enough of the conspiracy shit. Jesus wept, I don't know why the fuck you enlisted. You don't fucking trust anybody," McCoy snapped. He was close to tears at the memory of his fallen friends.

Dudek held his tongue, and a silence fell over them, each mourning in their own way.

That was when the first explosion rang out. The building shook, and the room resonated with the sound of the detonation. Smoke filled in from the hall, and by the time everybody rose to their feet, the echo of automatic fire was all around them. Bullets flew and war was declared.

The group emerged from the smoke, masks over their faces. M-16's sang out in chorus as they cut down the Marines in a storm of blood and gun smoke.

Dudek took a round to the leg and fell to the floor. A few moments later, McCoy fell on top of him. Dudek felt the rush of warmth as blood flowed down his back.

Slowly, the staggered Marines were starting to fight back. Tables were overturned and fire was sent back towards the group. Their attackers were dressed in full military gear, which made everything all the more confusing.

Dudek shook himself free from beneath his friend, and without hesitation, pulled his service revolver and opened fire. Someone's head explode in a puff, sending globs of brain flying in all directions.

A second later, another explosion rang out, and a flash of blinding light filled the room. Dudek tried to shield his eyes, but it was too late. The resulting shockwave from the thrown grenade threw him to the floor again. Pain overflowed him, his mind short circuited and for a while, there was nothing but darkness.

Dudek came to with the smoke still clearing and the sounds of battle ringing in his ears. He tried to sit, but couldn't move. All around him bodies lay in pools of blood, piss and shit. Bodies had been ripped apart by the blast, and while the worst of the damage had been contained to the mess hall, thanks to the security measures taken during the design stage, it was clear that the casualties were severe.

Omega-Base-Six was under attack, and it was an inside job.

Dudek hauled himself into an upright position, ignoring white hot pain in his lower half. He looked around and saw his friends all dead, what remained of them at least.

He tried to stand, and that was when he saw his legs. They were nothing but blood stumps. One extended further than the other, but the result was the same. Slithers of torn flesh, raw meat, and exposed nerves.

"Help me," Dudek called out as the pain caught up with him. "Somebody help."

Nobody gave an answer, but the footsteps that came from behind him were response enough.

"Do it," Dudek growled. He heard the gunshot, but did not have long enough to feel the pain as half of his face was blown off.

The attack in the mess hall had been well planned, but it alerted the rest of the station to the problem. Gunfire soon rang out across the entire platform, as the Marines began to fight back. The upper floor was placed on lock down. The automatic doors sealing the officers inside, along with all of the computers and controls that contained the entire base's central information store.

The hallways filled with blood, and explosions ripped through walls and decimated the inner structure. Smoke and flames filled the base. Alarms sounded and people ran in all directions. Nobody knew who was attacking, but nobody expected the bullets to come from people wearing the same uniforms as them. Men they had worked with for months, men they considered brothers.

Martin heard the commotion. He could hear alarms sounding but everything else was muffled. He thought he recognized the sound of gunfire. Still, he knew his lab was secure, especially with him holed up on the second floor.

Martin also knew of the storm. He could feel it through the walls, but it didn't bother him. He was too focused. The shark felt it also and was restless as a result. She was already over thirty feet long, and her growth was accelerating according to the data Martin assembled.

The lift arrived and the doors opened. The two men didn't wait. They flipped the switch and opened up the second level and were down the steps before the floor had finished opening.

"Who are you?" Martin asked when the two men charged towards him. The face masks they wore were speckled with blood.

"Dr. Lucas, we need to get you out of here. Omega-Base-Six has been compromised. We have been authorized to remove you with immediate effect," the larger of the two men spoke. He reached up and pulled his mask off as he did.

"Compromised, how? This place is a fortress," Martin asked, confused.

"They had men on the inside. A lot of them. We need to move now. Take whatever you can. We need to leave," the second man answered. He, too, removed his mask.

"General Burke, sir. I … give me thirty seconds." Martin began to rush around the computers, copying and transferring the data.

"We may not have that long, Dr. Lucas," General Burke said as he turned and stared at the shark.

"What about her?" Martin asked.

"Right now, getting you out of here is my main priority," Burke spoke as he grabbed Martin by the arm.

"General, we need to leave, now!" The other man looked around nervously.

"Move, Dr. Lucas, we can't wait any longer." A genuine sense of urgency existed in the man's voice, but no panic. The general, for all that was going on around him, was still remarkably cool.

"I'm ready," Martin spoke, grabbing more and more notebooks as he moved. "Where are you going to go? There is a storm out there."

"We have arranged something. The storm is unfortunate, but we need to leave this base. We are not safe here."

Martin looked over his shoulder as he was bundled out of the room. The shark was restless in the water, bucking and thrashing.

"We need to come back for her… I …" Martin stammered, but had no chance to finish his sentence for he was up the stairs and into the elevator before he could process what was happening.

As he rose, the sound of gunfire increased. For all of his years in the military, and the strange places he had been, Martin had never been in an actual combat zone.

"Who is doing this?" he asked as the two men beside him checked and triple checked their weapons. They pulled their masks back over their faces just as the doors opened. A fireball flew by the opening lift doors and Martin screamed out in surprise. His legs began to buckle but was caught by the two military men.

"This way, we need to make it to the boat," the larger man called to the general.

A man Martin knew, a young officer who was on his first posting, appeared. He was armed and looking around in all directions. His face was pale and his eyes wide. He stared at the two men, and at Martin who stood between them. Recognition flashed in his eyes, followed by the flare of the M-16 muzzle as it fired two rounds into his head. His skull split open like a rotten melon, and he fell to the floor in a pile of his own gore.

"What's going on here?" Martin asked as he was half-pushed and half-pulled through the middle of a firefight. They ran down the corridor in a crouch, ducking into the first room they saw. General Burke ripped an M-16 out of the hands of a fallen soldier and sent a burst of gunfire into the hall. A few moments later, everything fell quiet.

"We have been infiltrated. A terrorist cell managed to get people to turn on us from the inside. We need to get you out of here. You and your research are critical to the mission," General Burke spoke in a rush.

Their corridor was clear, but the fight was far from over. The scent of fires and the acrid after-twang of gunpowder hung heavy in the air.

"We need to move," the taller man spoke. He had a strange accent, or rather a forced lilt to his voice that made Martin think it was fake.

General Burke hauled Martin to his feet. "It's time to run, Dr. Lucas."

Martin tightened his grip on the notebooks and papers that he held. They were stained with blood from where he had dropped them.

"We can't just leave her. You don't understand ..." Neither man listened. They shoved Martin and once again they were off. The hall was quiet. Smoke filled the base as fires raged somewhere unseen. Bodies littered the floor. Limbs separated from torsos, heads split in half or removed completely. Martin even saw several stray fingers sliding through the pools of blood.

Martin looked at the faces. So many, so young. He wept and allowed himself to be lead, as fresh sounds of war echoed from deeper inside the base.

CHAPTER 4

Special Agent in Charge Marcus Lovell sat in the plane, chewing on his bottom lip. The vehicle was a state-of-the-art piece of equipment that had proven it could fly in almost any set of conditions.

"Omega-Base-Six is not responding, sir," Randy Johnson spoke from the cockpit of the plane. "I think we are too late, we will be coming in hot."

Marcus sighed and checked his weapon. He had a P229 on one hip and an FN Five-Seven on the other, and his preferred FN P90 submachine gun sitting across his lap. The other five members of the team were similarly armed and ready to go. Only two had swapped out the FN P90 for Remington 870.

"We don't have a problem with that, Mr. Johnson," Marcus replied.

They flew in silence for a few moments, the plane cutting through the wind. If they had not known of the storm raging outside, it would have been impossible to gauge its severity.

"Touching down. Stay alert, this storm is something else," Randy said as he placed the plane in the same spot he had landed one month prior. The rear hatch opened and a blast of wind and rain swept into the hull. It screamed like a banshee, but the men paid it no mind.

Once out of the aircraft, everything became a matter of routine. They knew the location of the lab and the quickest way to it. What they had not foreseen was the submarine that was docked deep below the surface, or the contingent of men that had spilled from it into the base as a secondary wave to clean up the mess.

"Keep together, we move swiftly. I know this isn't what we signed on for, but we don't know who is on our side or not, so we shoot to kill," Marcus ordered once they were in the stairwell.

"Sir, they could be—" Walter Budowicz began.

Marcus cut him off with a raised hand. "Some will be friendlies, they will all be dressed like U.S. Marines, but we cannot take the risk. We are at war, gentlemen, and the rules are changing every day."

They moved down the steps and onto the upper level of the base: the superior officer's control room. It was a large open space, designed to act as a war room. If necessary, the United States could be run based off the equipment on the base. That was before it was shot to shit and drenched with blood.

Bodies lay everywhere, while the computers and terminals sparked and spat as they tried to work in spite of the damage they had taken.

"Sweet Jesus," one of the men whispered. He fished a crucifix out of his vest and kissed it.

"Eyes open, we need to get that shark." Marcus led his team through the debris.

A hand reached out and grabbed him around the ankle. Marcus kicked out at it and carried on walking.

The upper floor was sealed, as was the inserted protocol for any emergency situation.

"Damn, that means they were up here already," Colin Doyle spoke, looking at the bodies.

"How deep does this go?" another asked.

"We can worry about that later. Focus," Marcus growled at his team.

They fell silent, and Marcus grabbed his radio. "Professor, I need you to find us out of here."

"Give me two seconds," the voice came back. A heartbeat later, the lights dimmed as the power was taken down. The emergency generators kicked in, but the lighting was minimal. The doors buzzed and then unlocked.

"We're in, move." Marcus led the way and the others followed close behind.

The base was quiet, the groans of the injured and the dying rolled like a strange chant. Gun smoke hung in the air like a mist.

Ahead of them, a door opened. A marine stepped out, holding his rifle across his chest. He was covered in blood and walked with a limp. His leg dragging uselessly behind him. He looked down the corridor and saw the team of black-clad operatives heading towards him. He stared at them. His rifle twitched in his hand, but then fell to the floor. The man collapsed to his knees and stared at them.

Marcus saw the look in his eyes and froze. The marine could not have been very long out of his teens. He had dimples in his cheeks and a baby face that Marcus did not think could have grown a beard if he tried. For a moment, everything seemed to stand still.

The marine flinched, and Marcus fired a single shot from his rifle. The back of the marine's head exploded with a wet thwack, and the body fell to the floor, the concealed pistol falling from his hand as he collapsed.

Marcus opened the door to the lift and looked at his men. "I want the three of you to stay here. Stay alert, and remember, consider everybody a threat. Brown, Doyle, come with me."

As the lift descended, Marcus swapped the machinegun for his SIG; a few moments later, the others did the same.

"We need the scientist and the shark; remember, they are to be brought in alive. From this point out, this is a rescue mission," Marcus spoke as the doors opened.

"All clear, sir," Doyle called from the lower floor. "No sign of the scientist anywhere. This place is a mess though. Looks like there could have been a struggle."

Marcus came down the stairs and took one look at everything. "Nope, no struggle, just a unique interior decorating style." His eyes fell on the tank.

"Holy …" Doyle began to say, but ended in a whistle. "That shark is enormous. What are we supposed to do with it?"

"That depends on the status of the base. If the structural integrity is threatened then we are to destroy it; however, our orders are to stabilize the base, ride out this damned storm, and extract both the shark, and this Dr. Lucas," Marcus instructed his men.

"Sir," Travis Brown called down from the upper lab. "It's Fellows, he says they have a mark on the doctor."

"I am on my way. Tell him to engage, but protect the doctor at all costs." Marcus turned and left the lab. "Doyle, you stay here, anybody comes down here that isn't us, and you smoke them."

Marcus heard the fresh round of gunfire as the elevator finished its ascent. The door opened and the body of Richard Fellows fell towards them. His throat was missing. A burst of automatic fire sliced a whole the size of a fist in his gut. He coughed and choked, falling against Marcus, who had no choice but to push his dying friend away. Dropping his shoulder, Marcus felt the bullet graze his arm, but paid it no mind. He raised his Sig and pulled off two shots, both of which pierced the masked gunman's forehead.

"Move," Marcus instructed Brown. They left the elevator and looked left and right. There was no sign of the doctor, but his team lay dead on the floor. "Motherfucking thundercunts!"

"They can't be far," Brown offered.

"Split up. Engage and take the targets down. The doctor is needed, but I would rather see him dead than off this base." Marcus took off to the right, and Brown moved to the left.

Marcus moved as fast, his feet gliding over the floor, moving over the puddles of blood, body parts and shell casings. Omega-Base-Six was lost. Marcus's jaw clenched when he thought of U.S. Marines selling out their country and their souls to aid the terrorist-controlled Middle East.

His arm burned and he had to swap the Sig to his weaker arm.

In the distance, alarm bells rang, and a rapid thudding sound echoed like a distant stampede. Marcus moved but found no sign of the doctor. Marcus refused to believe he was in on the plan, none of their intel had suggested it. That means he was not alone. Marcus rounded the corner onto the third leg of the base's outer corridor. The damage here was extensive. Debris littered the floor, and the walls had been reduced to nothing but gaping lumps of twisted metal.

Another body lay on the floor gasping for breath. He was missing a leg, but somebody had applied a rudimentary tourniquet. It was a bloody mess on the side of his chest that was the real cause for concern. It created a strange sucking noise as the man gasped for breath.

"Sorry, hold on, I'll come back," Marcus lied.

Marcus found himself in the mess hall, and the thumping sound was even louder. He had an idea as to where the sound came from, and what was causing it.

The large freezer unit in the kitchen area only opened from the outside. The large walk-in was not designed to house anything that wanted to get out.

Holding his Sig at the ready, Marcus winced as his injured arm pulled open the heavy door. The moment the lock was released, he took a large step back.

Men and woman in uniform spilled from the unit. Seven in total. They were shivering, their skin pale and blue tinted. It was all they could do to walk a few steps before needing to lean against the kitchen fixtures for support.

"What happened?" one asked, confused.

"You got compromised," Marcus answered swiftly. "Are any of you hurt, can you move?" He looked them over. One, a female soldier, had a bloody shoulder, and the arm hung useless at her side, but for the rest nobody seemed badly hurt. "They are still here, we need to move. I want you four to head deeper into the base, sweep and take out anybody that gets in your way. You three, come with me. There is a scientist among them. We need him alive." Marcus repeated the orders he had been given, and without taking questions, he turned and walked away.

***

Martin moved as fast as he could. Men rushed past him, their rifles at the ready. They moved with purpose and without remorse. They opened doors and unleashed a volley of fire. It didn't matter if the room was empty or not. No chances were taken. They swept through the base like a plague.

"This way," General Burke growled, shoving Martin towards one of the emergency escape shafts.

"What is down there?" Martin asked.

"A submarine. We are getting off this place. There are some people who are very interested in talking with you, Dr. Lucas," Burke spoke. He did not break stride or regard Martin in any way.

"Freeze. United States Secret Service, put your hands in the air," Travis Brown called. He held his Remington at the ready.

"I don't think so," Burke's second-in-command spoke, pushing Martin in front of him like a shield. "You want this man, just as much as I do. I don't think you will take the risk." He smiled.

Travis Brown stared at him, adjusted his aim and pulled the trigger. The man shrieked as his knee cap was blown apart, reduced to nothing more than a bubbly clump of raw meat and bone shards.

General Burke had retreated behind the curve of the corridor. He pulled his Glock free and fired at Brown.

Brown took a round to the leg, but dove into a nearby room just as a second shot rang out. He rolled into cover against the door. He could hear Burke arguing with Martin. Brown leaned out from the door and fired. He shot wide, not wanting to hit the doctor with anything worse than a ricochet, but it drove them back, away from the exit shaft.

Burke held Martin as a shield, so Brown left the room and fired another short burst. He ran to use the corner of the corridor as cover, as Burke and Martin backed away.

"Help me," the injured man cried. His weapons lay beside him, but he was clutching his injured limb and had no mind to attack.

Brown ignored his pleas, but stepped on his leg for good measure as he passed. The man cried out for a moment before the pain allowed him to slide into unconsciousness.

"Sir, I've got eyes on the scientist. They are on the move, heading north along the outer passageway," Brown moved and spoke, his eyes focused on what lay ahead. His leg hurt but the wound was superficial.

"Copy that. I have some survivors. A team has gone deep, but we will sweep from our side. Keep your eyes open for anybody they have left behind. It's too quiet," Marcus answered.

General Burke pulled Martin backwards. His forearm was locked under the scientist's chin, and he was squeezing just enough to keep the doctor's air supply restricted and keep him subdued.

Footsteps were following them, close enough to give Burke cause for concern. He looked around and saw the stairwell. Kicking open the door, they disappeared inside.

"In here, quick," Burke growled, jabbing his pistol in Martin's back.

They made their way up the stairs, while in the hallway shouts and shots rang out as Marcus and his team came across the clean-up crew who were sweeping through the base.

"I thought we had a submarine," Martin couldn't help but ask.

"Shut up, there's been a change of plan," Burke snapped as he grabbed the radio from his belt. "The fucking spooks are here. Push off, we will follow in the bird. For the rest, the plan remains the same."

The response came, but Martin didn't hear it. The moment they opened the door to the helipad, the thunderous howl of the storm drowned out every other sound.

The plane sat tethered into position on the helipad. It was an enormous thing that looked like something out a superhero comic.

Martin couldn't hear the instructions he was being given, but when Burke shoved him towards the plane, the intentions were clear enough.

Randy Johnson did not see the men approaching the jet, and when the cockpit escape hatch was wrenched open, he had no time to react. General Burke emptied his Glock's magazine into the pilot's chest.

They were inside the plane before the doors to the helipad opened. Marcus emerged with two other Marines. They dropped to their knees to brace against the wind and opened fire. The bullets bounced off the body of the plane, doing nothing more than creating sparks that were whisked away by the storm.

"Do you know how to fly this thing?" Martin asked.

General Burke gave no answer but powered up the engines and disengaged the restraints that held the plane in place.

Instantly, the craft was pushed by the wind. "Shit," Burke growled as he struggled for control. A few moments later, they were in the air.

The group on the ground opened fire again and an alarm began to sound. The plane listed to one side. As the body twisted, the wind got under them and the craft was lost. Without an experienced pilot at the controls, it was a hard thing to fly on the best of days, and impossible in such conditions.

Martin pulled at the safety belts. He fell from the chair, but there was no time to escape. They crashed down onto the platform.

The impact was a jarring experience accompanied by the overpowering screech of twisting metal. The engines roared before they exploded in four balls of fire. They swept along the wings, and in seconds, the plane was ablaze.

Martin tried to move, but his leg was stuck. Martin was in pain, his body screamed as a searing heat consumed him, and then nothing, the soothing, cold embrace of darkness swept over him and washed the pain away.

The ground rumbled and the explosion that rocked the platform was deafening. It decimated the helipad, sending it crashing down into the control room below.

Marcus and the two Marines fell back the moment they saw the fuel start leaking from the plane's fuselage, but they were not quick enough. The stairwell they were in collapsed as the blast shook Omega-Base-Six to the core.

The fireball swept through the column just as Marcus hurdled the fallen bodies of two Marines. He tucked and rolled through the doorway, but he was ablaze when he came to rest. Rolling from side to side, he subdued the flames but the agony of his new injuries held him incapacitated.

Marcus was dying. He knew it. The same way he knew everybody on the base was dead. He smiled, his cracked and broken mouth curling upwards, as he realized everything was safe. The scientist was dead, and the shark was in its tank.

They had won.

CHAPTER 5

Five Years Later

The midday crowd clapped as the curtains were drawn. Destiny Head walked out on stage, her near-naked body shimmering with glitter, lotion and sweat. She staggered into the middle of the stage, grabbed the pole and let experience do the rest.

Truth be told, she had no real concept of where she was or what she was doing. The four lines of high-quality coke she had just snorted from the length of her husband's cock had her flying higher than angels. She could feel the music and her body swayed in response. A life time of working Vegas strip joints meant that, after a while, the body just reacted.

The club was empty, save for the hardcore drunks and truly perverted souls. Those who enjoyed watching the cheap girls dance.

In her day, Destiny Head, the name she had used her entire career, had been one of the best-looking girls in the club. She had the headline nights and peak hours. Her tight body and perky breasts had driven the crowd wild, and the tricks she would do with her vagina had them all wanting a piece.

The problem had been, she was more than happy to give them what they wanted. A few dollars extra in her wallet at the end of the night to let the odd customer take her out back and fuck her like a cheap whore was a fair exchange to a young girl running away from a troubled life. She had big dreams, as they all did at that age.

However, after twenty years of fucking and sucking her way through the night, there was nothing about her person that was as tight as it used to be. Her skin sagged, and her tits were all sag. All traces of their former perkiness was long since sagged away. The shape was gone from her figure, as her hips grew wider, and her ass grew softer. A worsening cocaine habit had started to erode her nose, and needle marks could be seen on her arms and thighs. She was not a heavy user, but when the needs must, or a hit was offered, she would take it.

Drugs were better than money when it came to her off-stage exploits, and there was always a man around who was drunk or horny enough to want to fuck her.

Destiny twisted her hips and rolled her ass as she hooked her left leg around the pole, gripped it with a strong hand and let herself fall. She spun around and around the stage, the public, a motion blur. Destiny smiled and laughed. She released the pole and stretched her body tall, her legs remained straight as she bent forward, reaching to take the bills offered to her by the three career drunks who sat center stage. All three men were long into their sixties, and neither would reach seventy with their lifestyles.

"Turn around for us, honey," one man slurred.

Destiny obliged, bending over, her silver thong pulled tight into her ass crack. One of the men leaned over and slapped her hard on the ass. Lynne gasped, but did not move. She wanted another, and maybe another. Spanking had always been a favourite of hers.

The dance ended and another song began. The rhythm grabbed her, as Destiny straddled the chair beside the pole. She tapped her feet and shook her chest. The silver nipple tassels swung in fast circles as she gave her body to the music.

Destiny danced, and when the music stopped, she left the stage, grabbed a long shirt and draped it over her shoulders, not bothering to finish buttoning it before she made her way to the bar. Not as a working girl now. She was off duty for a while. Now, she was a customer.

Destiny walked up to the bar and smiled at the bartender. "Make mine a double Jack, Tony." She gave her order and walked towards the man who sat at the end of the bar. He had his back to her, and the counter top was covered with napkins and scraps of paper.

"Coming up," Tony, the bartender answered, grabbing a glass and pouring a generous double.

"Hey baby," Destiny, whose real name was Lynne, spoke to the man. She leaned over his shoulder and kissed his cheek.

This seemed to break his concentration. He looked up and smiled at the woman. "You looked good up on stage today. I could take you out back right now and—"

"Easy, tiger, I'm just getting started, besides you just had some fun backstage." Lynne stood up and kissed her husband on the cheek. "What you working on?"

Paper scattered the bar, filled with scribblings and diagrams. Three empty beer bottles stood on the counter and a full one arrived a few moments later.

"Oh, nothing. I just, well, I can't explain it. I just have these dreams and ideas. I'm writing down what I can remember." The man took a sip of his beer, downing half the bottle.

"Here I was thinking you were trying to draw up plans to crack the tables at the Bellagio," Tony said with a smirk. He winked at Lynne who smiled back.

"Why don't you take a walk, honey?" she whispered in his ear. "Stretch your leg a little."

"Yeah, maybe. I could do with some fresh air and a smoke." He got up from the bar, carefully adjusting his right leg at the point where his flesh ended and the prosthetic began. He stretched and limped away towards the back.

Lynne watched him leave, and then downed her whiskey. "You want some, tiger?" She winked at Tony and they headed backstage. Tony was a much younger man with a steroid-jacked body and a temper to match. He had a wife and kid, but would fuck Lynne several times a week. He could shove his cock up her asshole, and she would only ask for more. His wife would never even think about doing anything so kinky.

They were not gone long. Lynne was not good at many things in life, but dancing and milking a cock were two of the things she did best. They returned to the bar, Lynne still adjusting her underwear, a glistening trail of Tony's cum streaking the inside of her thighs.

They found two men standing by the bar. They were looking over the strewn papers, leafing through them as if they were a public display.

"Hey, take your mitts off my man's work," Lynne screamed.

"How-do, gents? What can I get you?" Tony moved fast, leaving Lynne to disappear behind the bar.

The men were dressed in dark suits and looked as out of place in the strip club as anybody Lynne had ever seen. The men looked around, and then from Tony to Lynne, and back again.

One of the two men picked up another scrap of paper and looked at it. He nudged his partner and showed him the paper. The man nodded his head and smiled.

"Ma'am, we are looking for the man that drew these," he spoke with an official voice, but not the aggressive, belittling tones that most cops had when they swept through.

"What do you want with him? He ain't not done anything wrong," she growled.

"Ma'am, I'm afraid we can't discuss this matter with you. Now, please, tell me where the man is who drew these." The man stepped forward and offered the piece of paper to Lynne.

"I don't know. I didn't see who did it," she lied, and she knew they knew she was lying.

"This is important. The man who drew these—" the suited man started again. He had slicked-back hair and startlingly blue eyes, which stared at Lynne not with contempt or with disgust, but with something else, something genuine.

"He already sacrificed for this country. He almost lost everything he had, and now what. You want to break him down for a few god-damned drawings. You ought to be fucking ashamed of yourselves," Lynne growled.

The men looked at her for a while, and then took a step back, pondering their next move. Behind them, Tony still stood ready to take their order. What he had in muscles and cock size, he lacked in the brain department.

"It's okay, honey. Let them talk," a voice started up behind them. "I drew those things. Can you gentlemen maybe give me some answers about the nightmares I've been having these last few weeks?"

"Nightmares," Lynne whispered more to herself than anybody in particular.

The men in suits turned and looked at the man before them. He was overweight and had an unhealthy sheen to his flesh. He was sweating and his hands trembled uncontrollably. His body was crooked, leaning to favour his one remaining leg, while the prosthetic looked awkward and cumbersome. He had several bad scars on one side of his face, which both men knew would snake down his body, travelling all the way to his hip. They also knew that the man had burn marks over his back and evidence of the skin grafts which had been used to rebuild his chest. He would only have one remaining nipple, and two fingers from his left hand were missing, dissected at the palm. Everything was documented in his file. That included the surveillance notes and footage going back four years, since he was reintegrated into society.

"Martin Lucas. Dr. Martin Lucas?" the older of the two men asked. He was in his early fifties, his hair had started to grey, and had the sexy salt-and-pepper look that drove women wild. A day of heavy stubble covered his strong jaw, but it was hard to envision him as anything but clean shaven.

"I am Martin Lucas, yes. Not so sure about the doctor part," Martin answered. He looked from one man to the other. Something about them, their look, made his head ache. "Have we met before?"

"No, sir, we have not," the older man continued. "I know this does not make much sense, to any of you, but I am going to have to ask you to come with us, Dr. Lucas."

The men moved towards Martin, who took a reactionary step back. His head exploded in pain as another waking nightmare came to him. He heard gunfire and felt the ground shake around him. Somebody pushed him. He couldn't breathe. Guns fired, and he wanted to cover his ears, but he couldn't breathe. He was trapped, and it was hurt, burning hot.

Martin heard screaming, the voice was distant at first, but came into focus. Lynne, his wife. For a moment, the haze lifted from his mind, and he remembered the crash. He remembered the storm. There was a man with him, a military man. He remembered men in suits firing at them.

Martin opened his eyes. The men in suits were still standing by the bar. One held his wife with an arm twisted behind her back. Her bare breasts swung free as she struggled, as if they too were mounting a fightback, eager to hit anybody that came too close.

"Leave her alone," he cried out, charging at the men, his gait more of an awkward stumble than anything else.

"Dr. Lucas—" one of the men began, but Martin threw a punch that crushed his nose with a satisfying pop.

The man backed up, his face stained red as a result of the blow. He snarled and moved, his eyes burning with anger. The glass bottled cracked over his skull, causing the man's eyes to roll into the back of his head. He hit the floor amid a shower of broken glass.

Tony looked at Martin and smiled. "Run," he said as he turned his attention to the other, who was still grappling with Lynne.

Tony strode forward and pulled Lynne free. He moved in on the man, who backed up and pulled a weapon from inside his jacket.

"Fuck you," Tony roared, his rage rising through the roof. He lunged for the man.

Two shots were fired. Only one was needed.

The first penetrated Tony's face through his left eye socket. The eyeball exploded as the bullet passed through Tony's brain and out of the back of his head, leaving a bubbling meat hole the size of an apple. The second shot hit him in the chest. His thick muscle was no match for the speeding projectile. Tony fell to the floor, his body twitching as the final commands issues by his brain reached a dead end.

Martin grabbed Lynne and hauled her towards the rear exit. The older men had taken cover beneath their table, while the two girls dancing on stage were so high they had no idea what was going on around them. Their naked bodies glistened with sweat as they spun to the beats.

"Dr. Lucas, stop, that is an order, soldier." The command was lost to Martin, who shoved tables and chairs to one side as he fled.

The door to the rear of the building opened and two more men in suits appeared. They charged the fleeing couple. They tackled them both, and all four fell to the floor. Martin landed on his side, and he felt his shoulder pop out of joint. He growled in pain as he was twisted to his front and his hands were cuffed behind his back.

The second man had not been so lucky. Lynne had landed on her back, her legs spread. The agent's face hit her breasts, which filled his mouth. Jumping to his feet, he rolled Lynne over and cuffed her. It wasn't until he was done that he noticed the slimy stain on his trousers from where he had come to rest against Lynne's greasy crotch.

"Dr. Martin Lucas, you are being detained under the terrorist act. You do not have to say anything ..." Martin passed out not long after the first agent, the one who had killed Tony, started to read him his rights.

The last thing he heard were Lynne's sobs before the dark welcomed him once more.

CHAPTER 6

Martin came to, but had no idea where he was. His head was groggy, and he was being thrown around like a rag doll on a roller coaster. He was strapped down. There was a lot of noise, a constant droning din. Then reality dawned on him. He was flying. He was in a helicopter. He remembered the bar, the men that had come for him.

"Lynne," he called out, but before an answer came, something jabbed him in his arm and he was once again washed away into the cold arms of unconsciousness.

***

The room he was in was clear. That was the only word that came to Martin's mind when he opened his eyes. His head ached like a son of a bitch. He was sweating and shaking in equal measure and his throat was parched.

Martin tried to move, but he was held fast. Straps ran over his body and disappeared under the bed. Foam cuffs held his wrists in place, while an IV tube ran into each wrist, delivering fluids from two different bags.

He tried to remember, but his brain was a fog. He was thirsty. All he wanted was a drink. Somewhere in the distance, an alarm sounded. A real alarm, like a siren. Martin wanted to move, to escape and find his way back to his wife, but he was too tired.

He thought of Lynne, he remembered her dancing, and how she had sent him outside so he wouldn't have to hear her moans of pleasure as she was drilled by the barman. She was considerate like that.

He's dead now. Where's Lynne? I'm too tired. Martin's thoughts came in a jumbled bunch. He didn't have the energy to fight them. He fell asleep.

The next time Martin woke, he was still in bed, but the restraints had been removed. His prosthetic leg stood against the whitewashed wall. The two IV tubes had been removed but his head was still groggy. The sweats had gone, and while he still craved a drink, the water that stood on the table beside his bed was more than enticing to him. He wiped his lips with his hand and was surprised to find a thick layer of stubble covering his face.

Sitting upright, moving slowly, he tested his body. Everything seemed to work fine. In fact, he was feeling better than he had in a long time. Reaching out, he went to grab the glass. As soon as his fingers brushed against the receptacle, the door to this room was kicked open and four men in suits stormed in.

Martin jumped and dropped the glass, only to shatter on the floor.

The four men, who looked like they belonged in the Matrix, yanked the covers from the bed and hauled Martin to his feet. In spite of their rough handling, they paid respect to the fact that he only had one foot to be hauled onto.

"Move," one of the men growled, giving Martin a shove to keep him moving. He was held between two of the others, although they made him hop the entire way to the interview room that had been set up for him.

Martin was sat down in a chair on one side of a stainless steel table. A rod ran across the surface and attached to either end. Martin did not too to have the setup explained to him. The fourth man came in carrying his leg and he leaned the limb against the opposite side of the table.

"Where's my wife?" Martin asked the man, but he was ignored.

The four men left the room and Martin was alone again. He looked around, hoping to see something that would jog his memory. The room was about as non-descript as could be possible. Black-tiled floor, white walls and a white ceiling. One long plastic box light stretched across the ceiling. The decorations made the light seem much too bright.

The walls were bare, not even a window or a painfully stereotypical mirror with one way glass for more suited men to spy on him through. Martin had no idea what day it was, or what time it was. He could have been sitting at the table for five minutes or five hours, the concept of time was beginning to lose all meaning.

When the door opened and another man walked in, Martin almost smiled at him, he was so pleased to see somebody else.

"Dr. Lucas, good to see you awake again," the man spoke but did not look at Martin. He sat down at the table without making eye contact.

"Where is my wife?" Martin asked again.

"That is not part of this conversation," the man responded calmly, still not taking the time to look Martin in the eye.

"Where is she, asshole?" Martin could feel the rage growing inside him.

"She is safe. Now, if we can bring things back on track," the man answered, and pulled the conversation back on his preferred track with ease.

"Who are you?"

"Dr. Lucas—"

"Cut that out," Martin spoke. "My name is Martin Lucas, I'm not a doctor."

"Interesting," the man remarked, finally looking up to stare at Martin. "You really don't remember anything."

"I remember you kidnapping me. I remember you tackling my wife to the floor, and I god-damned remember you killing Tony." Martin's anger began to shift.

"I mean before, long before. You must remember that." The door to the interview room swung open, crashing into the wall behind the door.

"That is more than enough, Edwards," the newcomer snapped. "What the living hell is going on here?"

"Sir, I … we …" the man stammered as he jumped up from the chair.

The man limped into the room. He was leaning on a cane, but had an air of authority about him that even Martin could not ignore.

"Leave, now." The man spoke the two words in a soft voice, but it emptied the room quicker than a curry fart in an elevator.

The man limped to the table and passed the limb over to Martin. "I believe we have all gotten off on the wrong foot here, Dr. Lucas." He stopped as he considered his words. "No pun intended."

"I'm not who you think I am," Martin answered.

"Oh but you are. You are just not who you think you are."

"What?"

"You are Dr. Martin Lucas. You were one a scientist in the U.S. Military. In the bio weapons division. Does the name Omega-Base-Six ring any bells?" The man leaned back.

Martin looked at him, trying to keep his cool, while on the inside he felt as if his body was the inside of an overheating nuclear reactor. The man only had one eye, his right was a milky ball of nothing. His dark skin was covered in a litany of scars that made his face looking creased and crumpled. They spread over his face and down his neck. He sat his hands on the table, waiting patiently. They too were covered in scars.

"Omega-Base-Six ..." Martin whispered the name. His mind was clearing, he remembered more and more. "Where is my wife?"

"Your wife is perfectly safe. She was debriefed on the situation and is back in Vegas. We tried to keep her long enough to detox the drugs from her system but she refused. She is quite an opinionated woman." The man smiled, but with the scars surrounding his mouth, the expression was more like a grimace.

"She is that."

"Can we get back to business now, Dr. Lucas?" The man was friendly, but he would not be swayed.

"Why are you here, now?" Martin looked at the man.

"You remember?"

"A little. I remember people like you shooting at us, when we tried to take off." The man on the other side of the table winced. "You were on the base too, weren't you? That's how you got those scars."

Special Agent in Charge Marcus Lovell sighed. "Yes, I was, I was on the base. I was the one who shot down your plane. But oddly enough, I was there to save you. We couldn't let you leave. If the terrorist took you or ... your work, the consequences could have been disastrous." The atmosphere between them had changed a little. Martin realized he was no longer a true prisoner.

"Well, good job. You found me, you saved me, kind of, and now you can let me go back home. Job well done." Martin moved to push himself away from the table.

"I'm afraid none of this is that simple, Dr. Lucas." Marcus shifted positions on his chair. "What do you remember about your work for the military?"

Martin sat back and tried to think, but his mind was a black hole. He could remember the base, vaguely, and he had the vague memory of working in other places, but the specifics were hidden away. "I don't remember."

"That is not surprising. You were treated with biological agents that made sure you would not remember anything about your time." Marcus fidgeted as he spoke.

"You wiped my memory?" Martin spat.

"Not wiped, but quarantined. We have been able to map the brain and isolate certain periods of time with the use of biological nano-agents. The memories are there, but hidden from you. It was necessary if we were to—"

"Release me back into the wild," Martin interrupted.

"Of sorts."

Martin sat back in his chair and ran his hands through his hair. He was surprised at how long it was, but then, his last years had been a swirl of drink and drugs. He couldn't remember the last time he had a haircut any more than he could remember the giant shark.

"Giant shark." Martin shuddered as the memory came back to him. "A giant shark, I was working with a giant fucking shark."

"Very good, Dr. Lucas. The agents we gave you when we brought you in are working to break down the barriers we placed. In time, all of your memories will come back to you."

"How can you be so sure? What if they were destroyed by your nano-agents or whatever?" A strange sense of peace settled over him when he thought about the shark and his research. Everything was coming back clearer and clearer. The images and memories coming into focus too soon, too many.

"Because we have your doodles. The ones you made in the bar, and the ones you have all over the basement of your house." Marcus leaned forward. "We know what haunts your nightmares, Dr. Lucas."

Martin looked at him, but his words were muted. His head was swimming with images and memories. Everything he had seen and done came to him in a single coagulated lump. Memories and lost emotions hit him like a vision and made his head roll with thunder.

Martin looked across the table and saw Marcus rising, a look of concern on his face.

"Dr. Lucas ... Dr. ... Martin?" The words were drowned out, spoken from the bottom of a pool. Martin lowered his gaze, his eyes studying the bare metal table he sat behind. Blood drops speckled the surface. New ones being added every few seconds. Reaching up, Martin wiped his nose with the back of his hand. It was his blood. He stared at it for a moment. Nothing made sense to him anymore.

Martin jumped to his feet. His stomach cramped. He doubled over and vomited twice before falling to the floor.

"What have you done to me?" he asked as his body began to shake.

Marcus was by his side, holding him steady until the seizure passed. "Hold on, Martin. This is a perfectly natural reaction. It was to be expected after a treatment as intensive as yours. The memory walls we created are crumbling, your mind is being freed."

Martin did not remember anything else, because someone ran in and jabbed him in the arm.

The jab did not knock him out, as he had expected, but rather made him fly. He rose above the pain and above the people in the room. For a moment, Martin rose above it all, an out of body experience, but it was nothing like he had ever imagined it to be. It was over quickly, as some unseen forced pulled him back into the real world.

The memories had returned to him, but now, in this spiritual form, he could absorb them. Everything made sense, and he was able to put things back into place. He was whole once more, as if somehow the memories made him solid. The more he remembered, and the more he organized them, the closer to his real body he sank.

Martin came to. He was back in bed, but sitting up. He was still in the vomit-stained hospital gown, but a pile of clothes on the chair beside his bed and a pre-packed turkey and stuffing sandwich stood on the nightstand beside a bottle of spring water and a can of coke.

Getting out of bed was easy, too easy. He looked down at his leg. His clunky old prosthetic limb had been replaced by something that actually looked, and moved, like the real thing.

He head was clear as he got dressed and ripped open the sandwich. Martin grabbed the two halves with both hands and shoved them into his mouth, taking large bites, chewing four times and then swallowing, so he could take another bite. He was ravenous. He opened the water bottle and drank the contents down in one long take, and then sat back on the bed. His stomach was aching, but his spirit was lost in song.

Martin showered, using the basic, box-like space the room provided. The shower reminded him of the sort of cubicle you would find in a caravan. Which in turn made him think about holidays he had taken as a child. This brought his thoughts of his life and back to the military. He remembered everything. The clarity was as bright as if they had happened only moments before.

Martin's new leg allowed him to move with a far more natural gait. His steps were sure and his balance was possibly even better than before he had lost the limb, but clumsiness had always been a part of his character.

Dressed in clean clothes, not military, but also not your average high-street fashion apparel, Martin left the room and found himself in a long corridor, the layout not dissimilar to a hotel, if it was not for the clean and clinical decorating style.

The instructions that had been left for Martin had been clear. 'Get ready and come find me.'

Martin assumed the man with the scars had written the note. Marcus, something or other. But he could not be sure. The instructions, while brief, had failed to give any indication as to where the finding was to take place, and so Martin turned to the left and started walking. He would either find the man, or he would find someone else who could take him to him.

The hallway ended with a stairwell, which placed Martin in the middle of a throng of military personnel. The general hum of conversation was at deafening blast after the silence of his room.

After so many years of being lost, the sudden charge of military banter was a welcome event.

Martin stood a while, watching the uniformed men and women walk around. Marcus was leaning against the wall opposite the stairwell waiting for Martin to arrive.

"That took you a while," he said with a smile.

"Yeah, well, this new leg, as marvelous as it is, took a little bit of getting used to," Martin replied.

The two men looked at each other. "Thanks," Martin added, deeming courteousness to be the correct response.

"You and I are a lot alike, Dr. Lucas," Marcus began as they started to walk against the flow of general traffic.

"What do you mean, old and beat up?" Martin laughed.

"Something like that. Something like that indeed." Marcus smiled, a genuine smile, and a laugh soon followed. The two old men, both crippled by their years of service stopped walking and took the time to laugh like two schoolboys hearing someone use the word, member, in a sentence.

Nobody paid them any mind. On a busy base, they were merely faces in the crowd. Nobody understood the role the two men played in everything that was going on.

"I just mean that you and I are old warhorses. Not too many grunts like us still around. We remember what the world was like in the time before the biological warfare really began. We remember the Middle East conflict and the Syrian war. So long ago now. So much has changed." They had started walked again, stopping only so that Marcus could use a key card to open a set of large double doors.

The buzz of life fell silent as the doors closed behind them.

"Welcome to the United States Secret Service wing, Dr. Lucas."

"You have to share quarters now. I thought you folks were special," Martin joked.

"Oh, this is just a front. Everybody is beneath us. Besides, this is just a satellite station. To be honest, after the Omega-Base-Six incident, things changed." Marcus looked at Martin. It was not a look of malice or even of pity, but simply a look, which made clear the pressure and the weight both men needed to feel; a weight that was shared, borne through experience, and supported by memories.

"You know, I still don't actually know what happened on the base. I mean, I remember, but well, everything went down so fast, and after the crash, well my life changed, and I wasn't privy to the real news and current events. If you know what I mean." Martin had been hoping to use the conversation as an opportunity to gain some insight and possibly even closure on the events that led to his second life.

"Yes, it was a wake-up call for us all. Terrorists had infiltrated the U.S. Military. These were men who had served their country. They had bled and fought, won and lost. They were compromised and brought over to believe in something dark, something dangerous. We were not prepared for a strike of that magnitude, and certainly not one which came from without our own ranks."

"So what changed?"

"Everything."

"Everything?"

"Everything, and nothing." Marcus continued to lead them through the building. There were several rooms and staircases that they passed, but they seemed to be heading towards the back. "To the outside world, the events out on Omega-Base-Six were a tragedy, just like 9/11, or the Afghanistan Nipah attacks. The real shake up happened behind the scenes. Behind even the ones you and I know of. Protocols were tightened, everything we do now is monitored. Our every communication is checked and double checked. The cost of running the military tripled, but everybody, even the public were in agreement. People may hate politicians, but they sure do love an open and honest veteran talking about everything he sacrificed for his country."

They had reached the end of the hall, where an unfinished staircase led them down one further level. Martin followed as they found themselves in a basement area that served as a locker room.

"What are we doing down here?" Martin asked, looking around at the rows of lockers. To his left was a large gun cage that ran half the length of the back wall. Weapons of all shapes and sizes sat neatly in position, just waiting for someone to come along and take one.

"I'm getting my jacket, it's cold outside," Marcus answered. He closed his locker door and turned towards Martin. "Here, catch. You're going to need this."

Martin caught the jacket and slid into it without question. A few moments later, they were walking through the changing area and leaving through an old fire door.

They were in an alley. Snow was falling in thick flakes, giving the ground a cloud-like texture. The cold caught Martin by surprise. "The weather was not like this in Vegas," he said as he shoved his hands in his pockets. "Where are we going?"

"There is a small café not far from here. Normally, we would take the car, but in this weather, the streets are just madness come to life. Besides, the walk will do some good. You've been cooped up inside for almost a week and a half." Marcus dropped that bombshell as they started to walk.

"You know, that doesn't surprise me," Martin said as he and Marcus moved through the alley towards a busy-looking street.

They left the alley and were suddenly on a busy street. Cars whizzed by in every direction, people walked and talked in a mass. Armed with a mixture of briefcases, shopping bags and backpacks, all corners of society seemed to be represented. The central commonality between them was the red take-out coffee cup.

"Nobody told me we were in Washington," Martin spoke after studying the streets and the people passing him by.

"Good eye." Marcus looked over at him and smiled. "Where else would you expect us to be?"

"Good point."

Nobody batted an eye as the two men slipped into the crowd and moved along with the current. Four blocks later, away from the main road and still-crowded sub-street, they reached the destination Marcus had them aiming towards. A greasy spoon that did the name proud. A row of snow covered tables stood outside. Nobody in their right mind would brave the crazy winter weather.

The café was quiet and unassuming, but as soon as the door opened, and an elderly man appeared, the sounds of a thriving customer base spilled through the open door.

"Morning," the man said with a smile. Wrapped up in a thick jacket, which looked to be covering another, smaller jacket, with a woolen hat on his head and thick gloves on his hands, the older man, who must have been seventy if he was a day, gave them both a nod and set off back into the cold.

"After you," Marcus opened the door and Martin walked inside.

The café was warm and bustling. The majority of the people were standing in line, their jackets and hats still firmly in place while they waited for their take-away coffee, and probably more than a few of the café's trademark fried breakfast sandwiches. Martin had no idea whether they tasted as good as they looked, but the sign above the counter made a convincing argument. Martin's stomach grumbled.

"Over here, let's take a seat." Marcus led them to the left and through to the back of the café.

A small corridor ran along the other side, behind the counter, and presumably the kitchen. On the other end was a generous seating area with a classic diner motif. Booths with faux-leather seats and plastic tables with a chrome edging. The central tables were not in a booth format but had chairs in groups of either two or four with the same red finishing. Three of the eleven tables were occupied. One by an elderly couple who were eating their way through a breakfast that overflowed the plate. The other was occupied by an Asian couple. Both had large cameras around their neck and were each sitting with their eyes glued onto individual tablets.

An older woman in a green uniform with a white(ish) apron stood pouring coffee into their cups. She was completely unnoticed, and unthanked.

"Quite a difference, don't you think?" Marcus said as they sat down.

"I was thinking exactly the same thing," Martin said with a smile. He looked at the elderly couple who sat opposite one another, and spoke and laughed. The husband sat with his hand cupping his wife's. The younger couple were distant, lost to one another. "They could be strangers."

"Why are we here?" Martin asked as he studied the menu.

"Just to talk. We have a lot of things to discuss," Marcus replied. He did not take a menu.

The waitress approached the table. She smiled at them as she pulled the order pad from her pocket. "Morning, gents, what can I get you?"

Marcus looked at Martin, who had also closed his menu and slid it back into the holder that was attached to the wall of their corner booth.

"I'll take two fried breakfast sandwiches, an extra portion of bacon and coffee, thank you," Marcus ordered and looked over at Martin who was staring at him with a mixture of admiration and disgust.

"I'm hungry," he said with a smile.

"Me too, I'll have what he's having." Martin smiled at the waitress.

"Okay, coming right up. How do you boys take your coffee?"

"As black as my soul," Martin answered first. The waitress laughed.

"Sure thing," she turned around and walked away.

Martin waited until she was gone before he spoke again.

"You were saying," he said, trying to bring the conversation back on track.

"Five years ago, you were working on a project on Omega-Base-Six. General Walter Burke commissioned you to develop a biological weapon—"

"A Megalodon. I remember." Martin couldn't help but cut the man off. Not because he wanted to steal his thunder, but because he needed to hear the words come from his own mouth. So much had happened to him in the intervening years, he needed to convince himself that certain aspects were actually true.

"Yes. As I am sure you remember, General Burke was one of the men who turned his back on our country." As he spoke, Marcus raised a hand and allowed his fingers to trace the scars that ran over his face. The motion was a subconscious act, but a tell that Martin read and stored for future use. He was not the only one affected by the ghosts of Omega-Base-Six.

"I remember that too." Martin was patient. Happy to deal with things in small bursts, for he was sure that as soon as they entered the territory that came after his accident, he would need the time to adjust his mind.

"What if I told you that he was funding you with terrorist cash? That the Megalodon, the entire project, was designed by those in control of the Middle East." Marcus lowered his voice as they spoke.

"You mean I was working for—"

His words fell silent when the waitress arrived with their coffees. "There's free refills on those too," she said with a smile and walked away.

"I was working for terrorists?" Martin struggled to keep his voice down.

"In essence, yes." Marcus nodded.

"Is that why you came to collect me in Vegas? Why, after all this time?" Martin's head was spinning at a thousand miles an hour. Everything he had known for so long had been pulled away from under him. His life, his second life, a fake existence created for him had ended. The very substance of everything he was and understood had been changed.

"No, no, not at all. We know that you were set up. You did what you did for all of the right reasons. I have no reason to believe that you ever did anything that was not for the good of the United States. To be honest, had we acquired a real Megalodon, we would have entertained similar plans." Marcus sat back in the booth and smiled, looking over Martin's shoulder.

Their food arrived and both men dove into their plates. The sandwiches were everything Martin had expected and hoped for. The extra bacon was crispy and the coffee both hot and strong.

After finishing the first sandwich in silence, Martin could not wait any longer. Before starting his second, he re-instigated that conversation.

"I think you want me to do my project again. For you?"

"No, Dr. Lucas. You have this all wrong. I do not want you to help build me a weapon." Marcus finished his first sandwich and emptied his coffee cup.

"Then what is this all about? You take me from my home, separate me from my wife." Martin was growing frustrated.

The Asian couple had left, and the elderly pair were preparing to pay their bill. For the rest, they were alone.

"Keep your voice down. I brought you back because we need your help. It's Omega-Base-Six and, well ... just take a look at this." Marcus reached into his jacket pocket. He pulled out a small tablet and slid it across the table top.

Martin took the tablet and wiped his finger over the screen. A video loaded. That quality was grainy, shot from a distance and zoomed in, but Martin could make out the image just fine. His fingers were shaking and sweat streaked his face as the burned-out ruins of Omega-Base-Six floated across the screen.

"What is this?" he started to ask, unable to take his eyes from the screen.

"Just watch it. Then you will understand."

Martin pulled his eyes away from the base, studying the full scene as is played out. The tug lines, and the boat that was pulling the base along.

The ocean looked calm, until all of a sudden a wall of water erupted around the boat. As if the water was flash boiling. When the water calmed once more, the boat had been broken in half. The front section of the boat floated away, bobbing on the water. The rear portion slowly dipping beneath the waves before disappearing in a single, sudden tug. Something had pulled beneath the surface so fast the camera footage barely managed to capture the movement.

"What was that?" Martin asked, looking over at Marcus, who was finishing his second sandwich and starting on the bacon plate.

"You tell me, Dr. Lucas," Marcus replied.

Martin sat back in his chair, coffee in hand. He took a long deep breath. "You think my shark did this." It wasn't a question, but a statement. Albeit one Martin needed time to process.

Marcus nodded.

"Why are you telling me this, and why here, in a greasy spoon, and not in some interrogation room? None of this makes any sense." Martin was confused, and given the deception he had been part of five years before, he had developed sudden trust issues.

"Well, this is not exactly a matter of public record. The incident was covered up and only those that needed to know the truth know the truth. As for why here, even since that night, I've been a desk jockey. I'm not out in the field anymore. I mean, look at me, I hardly blend in, and with only one eye, my aim is all screwed up. I was brought in because I was in the right place and the right time. We set up a small task force to try and establish what is going on, and I said I needed you. You know this creature, you made it—"

"Her, my shark is a female." Martin was not sure why he had to make that distinction, but the need to correct Marcus on at least one point was too great.

"After the incident, we lost track of the station. By the time the storm settled, the base had fully separated from its fixtures. You and I were the only survivors. I didn't know you had survived until I woke up from my surgeries three months after the incident. All contact with the station had ceased, and everybody had convinced themselves that the damaged had been too great. Records will show how Omega-Base-Six was recorded as being sunk. We were at war, the terrorists were spreading their borders and making moves on the African continent. Our attentions were otherwise directed. The plot on the base was part of a large-scale offensive and before anybody could make any moves to instigate peace, we were locked in a silent war." While they spoke, the waitress came and refilled both of their coffees.

She paid their conversation no mind; she had been privy to many conversations during her years, and had learned that the best thing for all was to keep quiet. She had seen first-hand what came from meddling.

"So what happened, someone stumbled across the base and thought they would return the damned thing to you? Saw some stamp on the outside, property of the U.S. Military, if found please return to …" Martin smiled, he could picture the scene in his mind.

"No." Marcus was serious and Martin realized just how so at that moment. "We received an emergency transmission from the site. For some reason, a computer unexpectedly came back to life, just long enough for us to pinpoint the location. The base was retrieved and what you see on the video was the USS *Chosin*. She had been pulling the base for the final leg of its journey."

"Where were you taking it?" Martin was watching and re-watching the video as Marcus spoke.

"Omega-Base-Six is currently settled fifty miles off the Hawaiian coast. The plan is for her to be scuttled in four days' time." Marcus sat back and pushed his empty plates away.

Martin did the same, pushing the last streak of bacon into his mouth while he played the video one more time. He had zoomed in on the *Chosin* and slowed the video down. He could make out the grey skin of the creature appearing through the water as she rose into the air. The fin penetrated the liquid wall, showing the direction she had been traveling in. Rising up from beneath the cruiser to come crashing down on its deck. He smiled. The movement was natural, how sharks hunted. Martin had not messed with the creature's natural instincts, only strengthened them.

Even with only a grainy image to guide him, Martin guessed the shark was over sixty feet long, probably closer to seventy. That put the weight close to sixty-five tons, if not more. Combined with the speeds he believed she could reach, the total force of such an impact was staggering. That was not even considering the reinforced skin that Martin had equipped her with. He took a moment and whistled as the numbers formed in his head. With over fifty thousand pounds of pressure in its bite and teeth that were close to ten inches in length, the hull of the stricken military vessel would have been no match at all.

"They didn't stand a chance," he said, more to himself than Marcus.

"Then you understand why we need to understand where this shark could be, and how we can take care of her." Marcus place a handful of bills on the counter, which more than covered their meal, and rose from the table.

Martin followed, and before long, they were both outside. They were walking back, their conversation turned more towards sports, a subject both men held an interest in without any particular deeply founded affiliations for one team over another.

The black town car pulled alongside them, and the window went down.

"Would you like a lift?" the driver spoke.

"No thanks," Marcus answered, his words short.

"I think you do, Special Agent. You too, Dr. Lucas," the driver said again, the friendly tone of his voice had fallen away, to be replaced by a far more authoritative one.

Both men stopped walking, and the car, which had slowed to a crawl beside them stopped also. The vehicle continued rolling just long enough for the rear door to meet the two men. The window came down and an old face peered out at them.

"Agent Lovell, Dr. Lucas, please, join me for a moment. We have much to discuss," the older man spoke. He was serious but Martin sensed no malice in his words.

"Yes, sir, Director Cove." Marcus stood to a stiff attention on the street, and looked over to Martin. "Dr. Lucas, this is—"

"Malcolm Cove, Director of the United States Secret Service. Would you please join me in the car? We have a long way to go, and I don't think undertaking that journey on foot is a good idea for either of you." The window closed and the door opened.

Neither man had seen the driver leave his seat, but he stood holding the door open for them, the smile back in place.

The town car was not quite a limousine, but had a double row of seats that faced each other, and enough leg room for the three men to sit comfortably. The biting cold of the street was replaced by a relaxing warmth inside the car, and soft jazz music whispered through the speakers.

"Director Cove, it is a privilege to meet you again, sir," Marcus began.

"I'm sure it is, Agent Lovell, but cut the ass kissing and take a look at this." The director handed them both a folder. Each one contained identical sets of photographs.

Together, the images made a series. They showed three boats approaching the now re-familiar sight of the decayed corpse that had once been Omega-Base-Six. In the second image, one of the boats had taken the lead, distancing itself from the others. The third image showed a shadow running alongside the boat.

"That's not possible," Martin spoke as he flipped to the next image.

The shadow was gone. On to the fourth. The boat was gone. At least, the boat as a single entity. What lay in the water was the debris of what had once been a boat. Fires burned in clustered patches on the water's surface.

"Oh, I assure you it is very possible, Dr. Lucas. What you are seeing captured on those images are the remains of a vessel that was carrying the explosives that were to be placed inside the base," Director Cove spoke in a controlled and calm voice. The relaxed flow of his words put Martin on edge. "So, would one of you like to tell me what the holy hell is going on? Why has this shark chosen now to reappear? Is this something we should be worried about?"

"We don't know for sure, sir," Marcus answered.

"Well, I think it is about time we got sure. I do not feel comfortable having a terrorist-funded super-shark running riot off the coast of one of our largest naval bases." The sentence began as calm as the last, but by the final word, the director was roaring like a woken lion. Spittle flew from his lips, and his face darkened to a thunderous shade of red.

"Sir, if I may—" Marcus began

"Unless you can give me the answers I am looking for, you will shut the fuck up. I do not know what has gone on, but back when I was an agent, this would have been classed as a matter of national fucking security. People would have been running around like blue-assed fucking flies trying to find out the who, what, where and why. Not taking a leisurely stroll and a greasy fucking breakfast. Now you two misfits are coming with me, and we are going to find out exactly what the hell is going on here. Are we clear?" The rage reached a crescendo midway through the rant, and after that, settled to a tone that cut through everything. The direct was a no-nonsense kind of man. Everything he said or did had a reason, nothing was wasted effort.

"Yes, sir," Marcus snapped, sitting back, taking the scolding like a man.

Martin sat in the awkward silence that followed. He was not feeling the same nervousness that Marcus was surely living with. Martin's mind was whirring through everything he could recall, all of the information he had been given since waking up. It was a lot of new and refreshed data to assimilate. The images showed that the shark was hunting the vessels. That made no sense. Martin had taken an ancient killing machine and turned her into something even more efficient, but he could not understand why his shark would attack ships. He had never gotten so far as to instill any military fashioned behavior in her.

Martin was lost in thought. He only roused when he began to feel the gaze bearing down on him. Raising his gaze from his lap where his hands had been tracing imaginary formulas onto his trouser leg.

"Is there something you want to tell us, Dr. Lucas?" the director asked. He had settled down since his initial outburst, but the tell-tale signs of stress were apparent. Deep lines gathered at the corner of his eyes, and every now and then a faint sign of a twitch in the upper lip of the man's right eye.

"I'm not sure, sir," Martin answered. "I'm just running through some things in my head, trying to figure things out.

"That's good. I'm sure there's plenty of rust to be shaken loose." The comment was enough to show that the man, while calm, was anything but ready to let them sit back and relax.

"Where are we going, sir?" Martin asked, knowing the answer, but wanting to adjust the trajectory of the conversation.

"We are going to Pearl Harbor, Dr. Lucas. We are going to your shark." As their conversation concluded, the car hit the highway, and their pace picked up. The jet was ready and waiting for them by the time they arrived, driving right out onto the runway. A short walk from the rear of the car and they were climbing the steps into Gulfstream G800.

CHAPTER 7

The interior of the aircraft was as luxurious as Martin could imagine. Large chair-style leather seats ran down either side of a central aisle. Three sets of four seats, at the front, and one at the back. The rear set was positioned opposite a polished oak cabinet with an array of drinks and liquors. In the rear of the craft was a kitchen and coat store. Two women in anything but military dress were standing ready to welcome them on board. In the center of the cabin were two more leather seats on one side and a long leather couch on the other. Three large television screens were positioned to grant a clear view from within each section of the cabin. Everything had a polished wooden finish that matched well with the cream-colored leather.

Martin and Marcus fell into the foursome of seats on the left-hand side of the cabin as they entered, while Director Cove and his driver moved to the rear. They were joined by two other men both of whom paid no mind to the two men they walked by.

The plane took off a few moments later, and before either of them had truly been able to process what was happening, Martin and Marcus were soaring above the clouds on their way to Hawaii to confront a giant shark.

"I need a drink," Marcus said as he got to his feet. He paused and looked at Martin.

The expression on his face was easy to read. He was stuck. Caught part way between asking his companion if he wanted a drink, and sitting down himself, not wanting to tempt a recovering alcoholic.

"You're fine. I think that was linked to my other life somehow. I don't even want a drop." Martin smiled.

Marcus helped himself to a large scotch and was resoundingly ignored by the group that sat in the four-seat booth opposite the makeshift bar. They spoke in hushed voices that he could not hear above the sound of the engines.

"What are you thinking?" he asked Martin as he fell back into his seat.

"A whole number of things. My mind is going a thousand beats a minute. It's all been a bit of a mind fuck, quite literally in actual fact." He looked at Marcus, but continued talking. "I'm thinking about what happened, back on the base five years ago. I remember the crash, and I remember my experiments, but some details are still hazy. I'm also thinking about my wife. You never told me where she was."

Marcus took a drink and settled into the seat. "She is safe. She was cleaned up, the same as you, and debriefed on what had happened. We made her a very wealthy lady and gave her the choice of where she wanted to go."

Martin tried to imagine what Lynne would be like clean. He hoped she would be able to walk away from the demons that had chased her for so long. "Where did she go?"

"Florida. She took the detox well, and the news about you. She said she wanted to spend her years in the sun. For what it's worth, fully dressed and off the drugs, she's an attractive woman," Marcus offered.

"Yeah, she was. I could always see through the façade. I knew the real Lynne. She had a crappy life, and well, I didn't know who I was. I guess we were both tortured by our pasts. She did what she did to forget, and I drank because I couldn't remember."

"When this is over, you can go back to her, you know that." Marcus finished his drink and set the glass on the table that emerged from the wall.

"I know, and I will. I just hope she stays clean." Looking back with a sober eye, Martin realized he loved the woman he had found, but he couldn't go back to living the life he had. "What about you? You married with a family?"

Both men were eager to avoid the real conversation they needed to have, but were equally aware that the time for such talk was drawing ever closer.

"Nope. I was, once. After the accident, he just upped and left. I was still in the hospital when he came in and handed me the ring back. Turned out the whole sickness and health thing didn't apply to him." Marcus gave a laugh that was clearly forced and swirled the ice cube in his empty glass.

"Fuck him then, man, his loss." Martin tried to smile, but could not. The time had come to discuss more important issues. "I've been thinking about the shark." He lowered his voice, not wanting to share his ideas with the others just yet.

"I was hoping you had." Marcus sat forward in his chair, the pained look gone from his face. He was back to business mode.

"She is protecting the base. That is why she attacked those ships. She views the base as hers. Her territory is being threatened." Martin held his new found friend's gaze.

Marcus remained quiet, giving Martin the room he needed to explain himself.

"For some reason, she is connected to the base. Something is drawing her back, but I just don't know what. When the base was threatened, by the time she understood what was going on, she was left with no choice but to turn on the boats. To her, they were just prey at that point."

"What do we need to do?" Marcus asked, expanding the conversation.

"Before the … incident on the base, I injected her with a biological enhancement chip. Using the technology I embedded in the processors, I could essentially access the creature's brain waves and guide her, in a fashion."

Marcus coughed at the news. "You mean like a remote control?"

"Kind of. I couldn't fully override its brain, that would be close to impossible. What I could do was override the basic elements. I could guide her, target her anger and aggression, give direction to her rage. I mean, everything was just in the preliminary phase, and I have no idea what the results would have been." Martin slipped into a familiar comfort zone as he talked about his work, everything coming back to him in a fluid string of thought and expression.

The more his brain ran through the process of converting thoughts into words, the stronger his hypothesis began to feel.

"What does this mean? How can we use this?" Marcus asked, eager to form a plan to present to the director. Ever since the night on Omega-Base-Six, Marcus had been used as somewhat of a scapegoat for the whole affair. He had been the team lead, and one of his agents had double-crossed them also. He was not to blame, but at the same time, the buck stopped with him. That was always the risk of his job. Marcus accepted that when he signed the contract, and ever since had been looking for something to work his way back into the good graces of the institution he believed in with all of his heart and soul.

"I don't know. If I could somehow access to the chip, maybe I could steer her somewhere, towards a trap or something. We could capture her, and I could, maybe I could finish what I started." With his final statement made, Martin sat back. He had planted the seeds for something he himself did not yet fully know he was ready for, but something was itching inside him. That old familiarity, the career he had dedicated himself to.

"You remind me of me," Marcus spoke with a laugh. "So when we land, we will make arrangements for you to have access to a machine and what, you try to hack into the chip or something?"

"I'm afraid things will not be that simple." Martin stared at Marcus.

"I had a feeling you were going to say that." Marcus looked over his shoulder at the four men in the rear of the craft.

They had finished their meeting and were standing around the bar, drink in hand. Marcus had a bad feeling about the way they were standing around, but he could not let himself to become distracted by the games played out far above his paygrade.

"I think that she is territorial for the base because that is where the signal is coming from. She will have a residual memory that she associates with." The plane bounced around as they hit a patch of turbulence.

"What are you saying?"

Martin swallowed hard. He had a grip on the seat as the plane continued to bounce. He closed his eyes as his brain flashed images to him of his final moments on the base. The crashed plane, the flames and the smoke as he lay trapped in his seat. Shards of metal had sliced through his leg, trapping him like a wounded animal. He remembered being covered by blood and feeling his skin tearing away inch by inch around his leg. The plane settled down, and Martin opened his eyes. He hadn't realized how hard he had been squeezing the seat. His hands ached, and his eyes stung with sweat.

"We need to go back to the base. The control unit is locked away in a secret compartment, and without that chip, we don't stand a chance of controlling her." Martin felt his mouth dry up.

A few moments later, they began their descent. Martin looked out of the window, watching the islands grow beneath them. He then looked further afield, and in the distance, looking too tiny and unimpressive, was the husk of Omega-Base-Six.

Neither man spoke, they had no need for words. They both saw the remains of the structure. They both understood what was being asked of the other. All they could do was hope everything went without a hitch.

CHAPTER 8

The car that was waiting for them at the airport could have been the same one they had used on the mainland, apart from one major difference, the smell. Unlike the town car from the busy city, the one that greeted them at the airport had a clean and fresh smell inside this vehicle. They rode with the windows open, watching as the beautiful world passed them by. The mountains, covered in a rich and vibrant green, with the peak of the volcano even further back. The blue skies and the warmth of the island had all three men feeling better. The conversation between them was even more relaxed than their fiery exchanges within the city limits.

"I could get used to living out here. Maybe when I retire I will spend my days in the sun playing golf and watching those hula ladies shake their hips." Director Cove looked at Marcus and smiled. "Do you play golf, Agent Lovell?"

"No sir, I have never had the fortune to play," Marcus answered.

"We will have to change that," the director said before returning his gaze to the world beyond the car.

The drive to the Pearl Harbor base was a short one. The longest part of the journey was moving from the preliminary security checkpoint over to the main building.

Once out of the car, the three men were escorted through into the main building and into a large meeting room where three other men stood waiting for them. Dressed in full-military clothing, the signals were clear. There would be no time to rest or to formulate a plan.

"General Kincaid." Director Cove shook the hand of a man of about his age, but with a considerably healthier complexion.

"Good afternoon, welcome to Pearl Harbor, sir," the general said. "I think it is best if we got straight down to business. The media are sniffing around wanting to know what happened, and to be honest with you, we are struggling to come up what to give them." The general directed the group towards a long oak table, which was already set with coffee cups in anticipation of their discussions.

"With all due respect, General, we are not here to give you advice on press relations. Dr. Lucas here is the man that created the shark." The general's eyes focused on Martin with an intensity that could not be ignored.

The general said nothing, but his face darkened in shade, with an expression that looked like thunder.

"General, I want to remind you that Dr. Lucas here was deceived just the same as the rest of us. He has been called in to assist as he is the only most knowledgeable person on the threat we now face." Director Cove was quick to jump to Martin's defense.

"Very well," the general spoke, but his voice was tense with rage. "Tell me then, Doctor. This beast of yours, is somebody using her against us? What sort of threat does she possess?"

All eyes around the table turned to focus on Martin, who decided at the moment he did not like the general, and would not pander to his bullying tactics.

"The chances of the shark be used against you via any, shall we say, third-party entities, is highly unlikely. In fact, I would go as far as to say that would be impossible. As to the threat she possesses, I would have to say, and forgive the technical language, you are fucked. She is protecting her territory, and she will attack anything that comes near her." Martin smiled smugly as the general's face grew even darker still.

"Forgive me here, but we are talking about a bloody shark. Why don't we just catch the fucking thing?" one of the other as-of-yet-unnamed military men spoke.

Martin had no idea who the man was, but his uniform identified him as Torres. "This isn't your ordinary shark we are talking about. She is a Megalodon. A creature that makes the sharks you know look like fluffy fucking kittens." Martin was building up steam as he spoke.

Beside him, Marcus sat back and gave a faint chuckle that he could not hold back. Martin had their attention, and he was going to make sure they understood who he was and who they were dealing with.

"This is a creature that I guess to be over seventy feet long, and around seventy tons. A killing machine designed in a laboratory to become an even better, even more effective weapon. She has skin as thick as iron, and teeth that could puncture the hull of any vessel you could think of. She will destroy anything that gets close to her, and she will do so without remorse, without hesitation. I assure you, Torres, by the time she has gotten through fucking with you, you would wish she was operated by the terrorists, because then you could have someone to direct your anger towards. But you can't. You can't because while they paid for her, I created her. I built her from birth upwards, in the name of this country." Martin's voice was rising, but he was not going to be made an example of.

"Then I trust you are sitting here with a plan, Dr. Lucas. You certainly talk like you have one," General Kincaid spoke, once Martin had sat back down and taken the chance to suck in two deep breaths.

"I do, don't worry." Martin smiled. "All I need is a team of men and a helicopter."

"That's all, such a simple list of demands?" The general was being sarcastic with him, and not in a subtle way, but Martin also knew that the best way to irritate someone of that persuasion was to answer them as if they were being serious.

"Yes, that's all we would need, to start with." Martin sat back and looked over at Marcus. His eyebrows were raised, his scar-wrinkled face creased even further by the combined look of shock and respect he wore.

"What do you expect to find, Doctor? We salvaged what was could already, long before we brought the base back to the harbor," the third uniformed man, Velasquez, asked.

"When I created the Meg, I implanted a bio-metric control into her. A microchip if you will, that allowed me access into the higher levels of her brain. Before everything went to shit on the base, I hid the central processing unit in a special compartment I had created. I believe the unit is still broadcasting in some way, and the Meg has picked up on this." Martin looked at Velasquez as he spoke, holding the man's attention.

"That is where you are wrong. There is nothing still broadcasting on that boat. We ran all manner of diagnostics checks before we commenced transport," General Kincaid answered quickly, and everybody could see how badly he wanted to smile, thinking he had gotten the upper hand in their exchange.

"No offense intended, General, but do you really think I would create something that could be detected so simply? That unit is on the base, and without it, we can kiss everything else goodbye." Martin held his ground.

"What makes you so sure?" General Kincaid was a man who would not readily admit defeat in a conversation, and Martin's adamant refusal to do the same caught his attention.

"Because, sir. Nobody will ever find my hiding space, and if they did, and the unit is gone, then we are completely fucked. Not like the high-end whores I'm sure people in your position are into, but rather the end of a long night, cheap skanks that leave you scratching yourself raw for three weeks after they do much as sit on your face and make you suck." Martin did not realize that he had risen to his feet while talking, but as soon as he stopped, he sat back down.

"I assume that concludes our business for now," Director Cove interrupted, moving between the two men who had been steadily closing the gap between one another.

"Yes, sir, Director. I will make sure a unit is made available to assist you. Please, freshen up, grab some clean clothes and we will meet again at fourteen hundred hours." General Kincaid was pissed and he made no efforts to hide that fact.

As disgruntled as he was at the interference, the three men walked away from the meeting knowing that even at that very moment, a team was being put together who would accompany them to the base. They would not be the very best that could be found, but the general would not dare to send them with a group of greenhorns.

CHAPTER 9

The Seahawk was sitting waiting for them when they left the main compound. Martin and Marcus were driven from the building in the company of Director Cove and two corporals who never said a word, or did anything to acknowledge the presence of their passengers.

A small group of arms soldiers were standing around the chopper whose engines growled as the two men approached.

General Kincaid was standing with the men and barked introductions.

"Dr. Lucas, meet Sergeant Greene. He and his team are the ones who will ensure that your sojourn onto the base goes without incident. Listen to him, and you will be just fine." The general looked at the other men in the squad.

"Good afternoon, Doctor." Sergeant Greene reached out and shook Martin's hand, and then turned to Marcus. "Agent Lovell, pleasure to have you joining us, sir. These are Privates Redmond and Eadie, and this here is Corporal Gunn, he will be your shadow while we are on board." The rotors had reached the peak of their whine. Behind them, the pilot gave the signal and they climbed into the helicopter.

They took off a few moments later, and by the time they had cleared the ground by enough distance to move over the fence that surrounded the helipad, they were moving forward.

Beneath them, the land change to the sea. A smooth pool of deep blue that glistened in the sun. The helicopter flew low and cast a long shadow on the water's surface.

"Watch your step when we reach the base. This old place had seen its fair share of abuse over the years. I don't want anybody falling overboard. This is a simple in and out and I have no plans to making it anything more complicated," Sergeant Greene's voice came through the headsets.

They sat crammed into the back of the helicopter. Despite the easy nature of the mission, the four military men were fully prepared for everything. Sandwiched between them, Martin and

Marcus looked not only tiny but completely out of place in their civilian clothes.

Neither man spoke. Marcus because he had nothing to say that wasn't already covered in the briefing he had given when they first took off, and Martin because he was too busy battling his own demons to think about interacting with the others.

"Take a look, gentlemen. Omega-Base-Six. I'm sure none of you are strangers to her history, both before and after. Now she is old, and she is fragile. Treat her with a bit of respect, like you would your own grandmother," Greene instructed as they circled around the enormous structure.

"I'd happily strap my grandma with explosives and send her to the depths, sir, but then again, mine is a cold-hearted bitch, so my view may be a little twisted," Private Eadie couldn't help but comment much to the amusement of the others. Even Martin managed to crack a smile at the joke.

"Very funny, Private. Next time she comes to pick you up and take you home, I'm gonna tell her you said that," the sergeant replied.

They flew another circle around the platform, tighter this time. As the chopper pitched to the left, Martin had a view straight through the center. The burned-out upper deck that had been the helipad came into clear view. The twisted shards of blackened metal, torn and sheared from its place as a result of his own actions. His heart thundered in his chest and a shudder ran through him. The sweat that slicked his skin froze against his flesh. His vision came and went in undulating light and dark waves. The Seahawk dropped lower, and he could see what remained of the control room. The rusted, weather-eroded remains of the computer terminals. Once powerful enough to run the country, and now, nothing but electronic corpses rotting in the Hawaiian sun.

"Dr. Lucas, are you okay?" the voice called to him. It was not much more than an echo calling to him from some distant corner of the world. "Dr. Lucas."

Martin pulled his eyes away from the approaching base. Everything came back into focus. The others sitting beside him, the helicopter, even the beat of the rotors above his head came through clearer. The whoosh of the blades fit with the rush of his beating heart. "Dr. Lucas," somebody was calling his name called again. "Martin."

The spell broke, and everything came back to full volume. It was deafening.

"I'm sorry, I was just … I um …" Martin stammered, trying to find the right words to accurately capture the sense of foreboding that had held him paralyzed with fear.

"Are you sure you are up for this?" Marcus was asking the questions. His voice expressed concern and his eyes confirmed that is was a shared worry.

"Yes, I'm good. I know what I have to do." Martin shook his head and wiped the sweat from his face with his hands.

"Good, that's good. Could you then please stop squeezing my hand like a woman in labor?" Marcus asked with a friendly smile.

"We can't land on the platform, the structure is too unstable. We will need to jump the final few feet to the deck. I want my team to go first. One you land, sweep for anything that may be a threat. Fire without hesitation. There should not be anything or anybody else on this boat. If there is, they are here without authorization, and that gets them an ass full of lead." The final instructions were given by Sergeant Greene.

"Doctor, once I give the word, you jump. Agent Lovell, I want you to follow him. I'll bring   rear. Have I made myself clear?" he called above the din.

"Yes, sir," the men answer in unison.

"Good, then move out."

The soldiers jumped the final few feet onto the deck. Martin could hear the groan of the station as they landed. Parasites arriving to leech off what precious little still remained.

"Are you sure you are up to this, Doctor?" The sergeant asked with genuine concern.

"Yes, sir. Once I set foot on the base, I will be fine. Don't worry. I know where to go. A quick in and grab as you said."

"In and Out," the sergeant corrected. "I hope your leg can take a sudden impact." No further words were spoken between the pair. Suddenly, without thinking, Martin leaped from the helicopter and landed in a pile on the metal grating that ran around the edge of what had once been the helipad. He lay still, face down, looking at the ocean far beneath him. For a moment, he froze.

A few seconds later, Marcus landed beside him. A little more graceful than the scientist, but both men were still alive, and that was a good starting point for mission.

"Move out, and stay sharp. Head for the stairs, but don't be overzealous. They could give at any minute. Remember, no accidents," the sergeant called, and his men responded.

They swept across the deck in a flowing, graceful movement, and Martin and Marcus were pulled along for the ride.

The door to the stairwell was long-since missing. The lingering essence of the fireball that had erupted remained, clinging onto the remains, even if the odor had been tempered by the smell of the ocean. The stairwell was wet and slick. Algae covered the walls like slime, sinking further down into the base, a slowly spreading grip that would choke the life out of the station. Omega-Base-Six had been claimed by the sea long before the plans to scuttle it came into being.

Marcus had no way of knowing if this was the same stairwell that had almost cost him his life, but the broken stairs, the fire damage. The thought alone was enough to make his skin itch and tingle as if still burning. He tried pushed the thoughts to the back of his mind. Knowing that they were nothing but memories, but he failed. They made the jump to the second floor and moved into the main corridor. Blood and death created a cloying aroma, one that no amount of sea breeze could conquer. Too many had died for this place to ever lose the stench of death.

They moved in a rough diamond formation, with Sergeant Greene at the head and Corporal Gunn at the rear. Eadie and Redmond took the flanks, trapping Martin and Marcus in the middle.

They moved quickly, walking through the pools of dried blood, faded to a dull rust on the dark-coloured floors. They swept the rooms as they moved; nothing more than a precautionary measure. Training put into practice, executed by the book with no room for change.

The sound of their footfalls merged with the groans of the base, as it was forced to take visitors once more. Every so often, a crack or a crash echoed through the halls, like some ghostly cry as some other part lost the strength to fight and succumbed to the inevitable.

Martin tried to shake the echoes from his mind, for mixed in with them came the screams. He relived the gun fights, and the death-dealing mayhem that had been the result. The gargled chokes of soldiers bleeding out around him consumed him, white noise that rattled inside his head and made it ache. His mind playing tricks on him, showing him their bodies lying on the floor where they walked. Some fighting still, reaching for their weapons, while others lay whimpering, floating in a lake of their own viscera. The terrorists had been swift and they had been ruthless.

Martin shuddered. He looked over to Marcus. He too was clearly struggling with his own memories. Marcus raised his head. He was sweating also, and the perspiration made his burns dance on his skin, as if beneath the surface of his marred flesh, the fight still raged.

"Are you sure you can handle this?" Marcus asked.

"Yes, let's get this party started." Martin tried to smile and failed miserably.

They did not need to indicate to the small squad where they were to stop. Even in the short time since the mission was conceived, the military men had memorized the layout of the base. Even though the lab had not been marked on any known charts Martin was easily able to guide the group to the exact location. The elevator doors had been pulled free. They were twisted and buckled, as if a great force had swept through the shaft.

They stood by the entrance to the once-hidden elevator and waited. For a few moments, Martin honestly believed that the lift would whirr into life and rise up to collect them. The reality was a quite different story. The body of the elevator lay at the bottom of the shaft, decimated by the jarring impact that had been the end of its sudden descent.

After the plane had crashed, and the retreat had been ordered, the terrorist operatives who were still alive on board the base had freely distributed the grenades they had acquired, wreaking a second level of havoc on the building.

"Give me a few seconds," Private Eadie spoke as he crouched down and pulled lengths of rope and clamps from his pack.

The experienced crew made short work of assembling the rigging that would see Martin and his shadow Corporal Gunn descend down into the lab.

"I've not done this in a long time," Martin said as he sat on the edge of the shaft.

"Don't worry, Doc, it's just like falling off a log," Gunn barked in a deep voice, his bassy laugh amplified by the elevator shaft he had already started to descend.

"Like falling off something, alright," Martin joked.

With a resigned sigh, he grabbed the rope, locked himself in place and allowed himself to descend into the darkness below.

Both men carried a flashlight, and together the beams were more than powerful enough to light up the base of the shaft and the lab that lay beyond.

The elevator was a crumpled heap. The cables had snapped as a result of the bomb and it had fallen to its demise. As such, a gap existed between the top of the unit and the lab beyond. Barely large enough for the men to crawl through, even after Gunn had been forced to leave the majority of his equipment behind in order to squeeze through the gap.

"Not like I'm gonna need much down here," he said as he unclasped his gear and leaned the pack against the inside of the shaft.

Gunn slid through first, followed by Martin.

The lab was a mess. Martin stopped for a second, as he realized he had truly believed he would be walking into his own home as if he had merely stepped outside for a five-minute lunch. The computers and machines, which had been state of the art back when Martin had first arrived on the base, were now nothing but rusted-up debris. Shards of broken glass and computer components littered the floor. The floor growled beneath their feet. The explosion had ripped long cracks in the floor, which, given the secret second layer to the secret lab, had not been created with the same battle-ready reinforcements the rest of the base had. As a result over time and the constant battery of the ocean and the rest of Mother Nature's elements, they had cracked and grown into a free-flowing spider's web of fragility. One wrong move and everything could collapse.

"Watch your footing, Doc, this place isn't stable," Gunn spoke just at the moment Martin had opened his mouth to give a similarly worded warning.

"Sure thing," Martin answered, picking his spots carefully as he made his way towards the stairwell to the second level.

A pile of notepads and loose sheets of data were piled in the far corner of the lab. Martin had been meticulous with notes, to the point of compulsion, his need to write down every thought and idea he had on the project. Once filled with such ideas and such misguided promise, now the sat in a pile, waterlogged, bloated with rot to the point that the pages themselves had started to burst.

"This way." Martin pointed to the hole in the floor that had, at one point in time, been the stairs leading down to the shark tank.

The lower lab was where Martin had spent most of his time, working with the shark, monitoring her. He had rarely ventured outside his lab, preferring to stay and nurture his baby. The stairway had fallen free from the hydraulics that had driven them. They lay on the floor of the lab, almost fully underwater. The second floor of the lab, which had extended beneath the area that most people assumed had been the lower level of the base, had been breached, and sea water had filled the room. Less than knee deep, the flooding was still an example of how fragile the base had become.

"We had better play this safe. Can you call in and check if the shark has been spotted in the area at all?" Martin spoke to Gunn, who stood beside him peering down into the lab.

"Good idea," Gunn replied. He stepped back as he grabbed his radio. Martin didn't hear the response. He had no real interest in knowing where his shark was. With the guard distracted, Martin lowered himself over the edge and fell down into the lab below. He landed with a splash, but kept his footing.

The entire structure seemed to rumble as a result of his sudden splash down.

Even through the entire lab was located underwater, Martin had never really been aware of the fact. Only now, with the station falling apart was he conscious of the power of the ocean. The pressure was so great it was almost a physical thing that had grown around him.

The lab growled as something tapped against the wall. Martin froze, his mind running crazy. The building was old, the creaks and groans were to be expected. Yet Martin couldn't shake the feeling that continued to stroke the back of his neck.

"There's not been any sightings. They've got the chopper circling, keeping an eye on things," Gunn called down. His face appeared over the edge a few moments later.

"That's comforting," Martin replied, just as the floor beneath him shook once more.

The tank was still intact. The glass was scorched in places and covered in layers of oceanic grime, but structurally it was sound.

Moving over to the tank, flinching with every crunching sound his footsteps created, Martin crossed the lab. The control unit, which was configured to the right frequency for the chip in the shark's brain stem, had been hidden into a compartment that Martin had created in the side wall of the tank.

Something bumped against the base once more. Martin forced himself to ignore the impact.

"Shit," Martin spat, as his fingers moved over the tank in search of the groove in the wall. He felt the tip of his hiding place, but the rest was blocked by the shifted computer console.

"What's wrong?" Gunn replied.

"The fucking computer is in the way. I can't reach the control unit." Martin grunted as he tried to shoulder the heavy unit out of the way.

Martin pushed with all his might, and the console shifted beneath his weight, but he could not get move the unit enough to give him the space or access he needed.

"Wait." The command was simple and followed up by a splash in the water.

Martin turned around and not surprised to find the corporal standing knee deep in the water. He opened his mouth to speak, but the groan that ran through the lab kept him silent. What began as a vibration quickly became a rumble.

"Do you feel—?" Gunn started to ask, but before the rest of the sentence was given breath, the floor exploded beneath him.

Metal screeched and twisted. The water bubbled up and the lab shook. A deafening crack rang out and the shark appeared, rising from the water like an apparition. The jaws opened wide, engulfing the bemused Corporal Gunn. They snapped shut with an audible clack, and then, as quick as it had happened, the shark was gone. The gaping hole it left behind was the only evidence of the event. That and the severed head that fell to the floor, landing in the water with a splash. It floated for a while, just long enough for the face to turn towards Martin, a look of eternal surprise etched onto the now lifeless features. Strands of loose flesh fluttered around the bobbing head like the legs of a squid.

The water levels began to rise as the ruptured floor began to tear even further. The water above the hole began to bubble, throwing the head around like a toy in a Jacuzzi.

Martin was frozen in place. His brain was still trying to catch up with what had happened, when suddenly the ground began to shake again.

He spun around in the water, twirling to the left and right, half expecting to see a fin rising up out of the ever-deepening water. There was nothing. Just an eerie echo of water bubbling as the level rose the final few inches. The designed buoyancy of the base made sure that the entire structure was still safe in spite of the rising water levels in what would technically be the station's basement.

Martin turned his attention back to the tank. The computer was still blocking the hiding place Martin had fashioned.

''Fuck,'' Martin cursed and slammed his hand down on the terminal. He raised his hand again and shouted as his open palm connected with the unit again and again.

Martin unloaded on the blown-out husk of what had once been his own workstation. Martin let everything go, his anger at the base, and at the people who had convinced him that his work had been for the benefit of his country. He roared and kicked out at the machine, as he thought about his life, and the second life he fashioned for himself. All of the rage that had been pent-up inside himself came spilling out of his body in a rush of anger as pure as anything he had experienced before. By the time he was finished, his hand was numb and the rest of his arm was tingling from the brutal assault he had unleashed.

With no time to spare, Martin leaped to one side, the groan of the lab breaking through the lingering red haze that clouded his mind, just in time. The shark burst through the floor, throwing iron and sea water in all directions. The computer terminal flew through the air and crashed against the glass of the tank. The creature powered its way through the hole to the point where even its dorsal fin had torn a gouge in the metal. Snapping and snarling, the creature thrashed its enormous body around, causing the entire structure to shake.

Its teeth were streaked with blood and strands of flesh and cloth that were stuck between the eight-inch-long serrated gnashers.

When forward momentum was no longer possible, the creature sank back into the water. Martin was trapped. He had jumped backwards, an instinctive reaction, but it placed him further away from the only possibly escape route.

Outside, the Megalodon crashed against the wall of the lab. It was a gentle impact, given the evidence of the creature's true capabilities, but it was enough to make the wall shake. It hit again, and again, circling beneath the base. Martin saw the shadow beneath one of the perforations.

He needed to move fast. With the computer terminal removed, flung effortless aside by the enraged sea-creature, there was nothing stopping Martin from grabbing the control unit. Nothing other than a mind-numbing fear.

In his head, Martin was calculating the relative force and speed of impact the creature was capable of achieving, but being close enough to it to hear its heart beat and the enormous, cavernous jaws snapping shut as they tried to clamp down on his flesh, was a different matter entirely.

Outside, in the distance, a burst of gunfire rang out. A chill ran through Martin as the sound echoed through the empty base. He remembered all too well how the shots had thundered on the night of the storm, when the base was lost. The nightmares would still wake him every now and then.

Martin pushed himself free and leaped over the whole his creation had so effortlessly created. Reaching with hands that were shaking uncontrollably, Martin fumbled his way to the control unit. It was still in one piece, and from an initial inspection, looked to be completely intact.

Wrenching it free, Marcus jammed it into his coat pocket and looked around. Beyond the wall, he heard the gunfire continue. The creature would not shy away from a fight. It is natural instinct was to attack. The only thing Martin hoped for was that it was distracted long enough to let him escape.

There was no need for him to leap across the other hole. There was enough room for him to work his way around. The only issue he had was how to reach the next level.

Martin looked around for anything that would provide him the necessary boost to reach the upper deck. There was nothing, but before could bemoan his luck, he was propelled through the air. The ground beneath him exploded, and the sudden rush of water shot him through the air, ahead of the snarling jaws of his attacker. Reaching, Martin caught the edges of the upper level and held on for all he was worth. Beneath him, he heard the crash as the enormous shark twisted its seventy-ton bulk and came crashing down on the floor of the lab, its full length stretched out to inflict maximum damage, to go for the kill. The entire lab shook and Martin found his left arm slipping out from beneath him.

The base, while not in danger of sinking completely, listed strongly to one side as a result of the impact. Martin kicked his legs as he tried to pull himself back up. Beneath him, the lab was gone. Close to the entirety of the floor had been removed by the powerful Megalodon, and beneath him, the blue water of the North Pacific rose, the surface still wild from the creatures attack. Beneath that, amidst the blue, was another shadow, one that was growing steadily larger.

Martin panicked. He moved too fast and lost his grip. He slipped and fell. He caught himself with his right hand, but his grip was precarious. The water began to ripple, and Martin tried to force himself to keep looking up.

The surface broke with a rush and Martin closed his eye. Something clamped on his wrist. Water rushed over him, and for a second, everything went dark. Martin was floating, he came away from the ledge and hung in the air for a moment, before falling with a jarring crunch onto the solid, albeit shuddering surface beneath him.

The world exploded around him. The men who rescued him opened fire on the beast, whose enormous body was stuck in mid-rotation when they struck.

Martin realized he was laying with his eyes closed. He opened them and looked around. He was in this lab, on the upper floor. His body trembled with shock. He heard the rumble of M16 but even that was not sufficient to generate any movement.

"Nothing," Private Redmond exclaimed, as he pulled away from the ledge. He was stunned.

"I emptied my magazine into its belly, but nothing. They just fucking bounced off him." He stared at the rifle he held in his hands, and then turned his attention to the deep water below.

"We need to move," Sergeant Greene ordered. "Redmond, help the doctor here back to his feet. I hope you got what you were looking for, Dr. Lucas, because we will not be hanging around for a second try." The sergeant tried to hide his shock at having finally seen the beast they were up against, and did so well, but his eagerness to be gone was not something he cared to hide.

"No, I've got it. I've got it here." Martin patted his pocket. The controller unit was safely nestled away in the pocket of his shirt.

"Great, let's get out of here." Greene turned the statement into an order, the three men moved towards the elevator shaft.

"Eadie, do you read? We have the doctor here. He is all ready to go," Greene spoke into his radio and gave the signal to Martin to hold on.

A few moments later, after another inaudible response delivered via the earpiece that the four men wore, Martin was lifted from the ground. He was hoisted up the shaft and greeted by Marcus, who was feeding his line through the portable pulley system, making sure it didn't slip and let Martin fall to his death.

"What the hell was that?" he asked as he unhooked Martin from the gear and lowered it back down.

"We made it mad." Martin's answer was enough to make Marcus shudder.

The chopper was waiting for them when they reached the helipad. It had lowered to the point of contact with the surface, holding itself a near immeasurable distance from the distorted metal framework.

As they took off once more, one man lighter than when they arrived, they saw the shadow of the beast as it circled the desolate base. Round and round it swam, not disappearing into the depths, and not rising to the surface. It patrolled its territory, like a champion. The first round was over, and the shark had emerged victorious, but the war itself was far from over.

CHAPTER 10

"What the holy hell happened out there?" General Kincaid was waiting for them on the tarmac. Words spewed from his lips, as the initial torrent of abuse washed over them.

"The shark sir, it ... it attacked the base while we were looking for the ... whatever it was Dr. Lucas here needed," Sergeant Greene offered his response, but the general was in no mood to listen.

"Did you get what you wanted, Doctor?" He walked as he spoke and expected the others to keep up with his fast stride.

"Yes, sir, yes I did. I got the control unit which will allow me to activate the chip I implanted—"

"I don't care, Doctor. We did it your way and we lost a man, a good man. All I want to know is, can you stop this menace before that beast destroys anything else?" The general turned to face the group, stopping in the middle of the road.

"I sure hope so," Martin answered honestly. It was an answer he regretted giving.

***

"You couldn't just lie to the man?" Marcus whispered as they made their way across the complex.

There were two cars waiting for them once they got away from the helipad. General Kincaid climbed into one, along with Green and the two privates. Martin, Marcus, and Director Cove got into the other.

"Can you really control it?" Marcus asked as the car began to move.

"I should be able to. But, she's a lot bigger than I expected. It shouldn't be a problem, but ... I just don't know," Martin admitted. "This was only ever a prototype. We never got the chance to try it out."

"You didn't tell them that, did you?" Director Cove asked, his tone flat and serious.

"No, sir."

"Good. Keep it that way." He looked at Martin and his brow furrowed. "What would you do?"

"Me, sir?"

"Yes."

Martin took a deep breath and thought through the options. It was a question he had been avoiding asking himself.

***

"She is drawn to the base. It was her home. She associated with it. We don't know enough about the Megalodon to say for sure how they would have behaved. People assume they are just like other sharks. The grandfather of all sharks, but that is not the case. She remembers, and she is protecting what is hers. I think the best thing we can do is fill the base with explosives, lure her inside, and blow the thing sky high." Martin addressed the group who had been waiting for them in the admiral's quarters on-board the USS *Theodore Roosevelt*.

It was a speech he had practiced briefly in the car, giving the same answer to Director Cove when posed the same question. Cove and Marcus were in the room, but were roundly ignored. It was Martin who was the center of attention, namely because everybody was well aware that it was his monster that they were fighting.

"Do you really think that will work?" Admiral Walters asked. He had lead the discussion, although to call it a discussion would be grossly misjudging the scene. The admiral was, for the lack of a better phrase, interrogating Martin.

"At the end of the day, the creature is a beast, and it is primitive. Effective at killing, but beyond that, it is simple. It has no rational thought, it has no conscience or inner voice telling it when something doesn't feel right. If we make that base irresistible to it, then it will work," Martin answered, confident in his plans for the first time since waking up in the hospital bed.

The admiral leaned forward on the rich red leather sofa, pulling away from the others who sat beside him.

"What about the extra abilities you have given it?" He was serious with his question.

Martin hated knowing the truth behind his recruitment, but this was a testament to his abilities.

"I gave the creature certain biological enhancements, that is true, but if you strap enough explosives to sink the whole Omega-Base-Six station, then she won't stand a chance. She's no superhero." Martin offered a smile.

The admiral stared at him for a while, and then rose to his feet. He smiled and held out his hand to Martin. "I'm damned glad you are on our side. If you were working for them on this thing all along, we would be in serious trouble right about now."

"The technical term would be fucked," Martin said with a smile.

The room fell silent, and the collective intake of breath at hearing the flippant comment was loud enough for everybody to notice. The admiral stared at Martin, and then laughed. To the palpable relief of everybody else in the room.

"That we would, Doctor, that we would." The admiral turned his back on Martin then, his attention directed towards to the general and the officers of the naval fleet who had been summoned to the meeting.

Everything happened so fast it made Martin's head spin. In less than two days, he had been plucked from the life he thought had been his, detoxed, had his brain de-fuddled, only to fly to Hawaii and be attacked by the giant super shark he had helped create, unknowingly for a terrorist organization that had complete control over the Middle East, and was busy with a biological war campaign on the African continent.

Martin needed to rest. His body ached from his adventures on Omega-Base-Six, and the stub of his leg was red and sore at the point where his limb ended and the high-end prosthetic began.

Rest was not on the cards, however.

Before the meeting was concluded, the admiral got a call that changed the state of the discussions they were having.

"That was SUBRON 1, your beast is attacking three of our subs returning from a training program. We've got reports that the *Charlotte* has taken a hit. She is still running, but the outer hull has been damaged. The *Bremerton and Mississippi* are in pursuit," the admiral spoke to the other officers in the room.

"Tell them not to engage." Martin jumped into the conversation, pulling away from Marcus and the director, who had taken on a much more back-room role in proceedings since they arrived on the island.

Admiral Walters stopped talking mid-sentence and turned to glare at Martin. "Would you care to elaborate on why we should not take an attack on the US submarine fleet seriously, Dr. Lucas?" He was pissed at the interruption.

"I don't think engaging her is the right move, sir. There is something else at play here." Martin didn't know what was going on, but something didn't sit right with him.

"Well, that is very clear, Doctor. Now please, sit down and let the big boys play." The admiral turned back to the officers, and once again Martin's temperament would not allow him to just walk away like a scolded child. He needed to raise his voice and interject.

"You don't understand, sir. How far out is the group? Why would she travel that far from the base, so fast, just to attack?" Martin was aware his questions were not really questions, but random musings, and when put together, they did not form a convincing argument for his suddenly pacifist view point, it was the best he could manage under the circumstances.

"Maybe your creature is being controlled by the terrorists. Maybe you are not as smart as you think you are, Doctor. I will not stand here and allow the United States Navy to be attacked in our own waters." Admiral Walters' voice boomed like thunder, and everybody in the room slunk back. Everybody apart from Martin, who as determined to stand his ground.

"Sir—"

"No, I've heard enough. The submarine group will engage the target, and they will blow it out of the water. We have pussyfooted around enough for one day. I assure you, Doctor, if sinking Omega-Base-Six would be enough to conquer your savage beast, then a host of CAPTOR mines and a few Mk 48's up its ass will do the job just as nicely. Now sit down and shut the fuck up before I have you thrown out of here." The admiral turned his attention away from Martin, who continued to stand his ground. "What are you all waiting for?" he roared at the room.

Everybody turned to leave. While none were involved in the combat that had just been arranged, nobody wanted to stand around any longer.

"Come on, buddy, we need to get you some air," Marcus spoke to Martin as he placed his hands on his shoulder and let him out of the room.

"He's making a big mistake," Martin said as he turned to look at Marcus.

CHAPTER 11

Captain Stephen Lewis of the *USS Mississippi* stood in the bridge of his Los-Angeles class nuclear submarine and listened to the shouts of those around him. Radar technicians were reporting back and forth with the other two submarines in their small group and with SUBRON 1 back on the mainland. Everybody was busy. It was good. Captain Lewis liked busy, because it meant nobody would have time to fear the beast that apparently lurked in the waters off Pearl Harbor.

Beside him, Lewis's XO Gavin Woods was busy relaying information down to the engine rooms. Their course was changed and speed adjusted to see if they would be able to lure the creature to follow them.

The *Mississippi* would take the lead and distract the creature, while the *Bremerton* would come through the rear.

The plan put together was rough and formulaic. Nothing like the manoeuvres they had been running for the past four weeks. The *Mississippi* would lay down some Mark 60's. The *Bremerton* would follow up with Mark 48's to take down the beast if it turned tail and ran. It was simple and effective. There would be no creature on earth that would survive such an onslaught.

"Sir, reports from the *Charlotte* are coming in. She took a glancing blow to the bow. They've taken on some water, but it is compartmentalized. They are on the surface now and are willing to hold position and play defence just in case." Gavin relayed the messages through to Captain Lewis.

"No, tell them to head home. We've got this fish." Lewis was calm and confident. He had served several tours in the Middle East and also several years off the Russian coast playing a rather dangerous game of surveillance with the Russian fleet, who for a while seemed to be harboring some reborn feelings of negativity towards the west.

"Yes, sir," Woods answered. He had been serving with Captain Lewis for three years and had been the commission XO on the

Mississippi for two of them. They worked well together as a team, and neither questioned the others judgement of situations.

"Sir, the *Bremerton* is in position," Oliver Maloney, one of the radio technicians called out.

"Thank you, Mr. Maloney. Mr. Woods, please give the order to take us down." Captain Lewis breathed out a long audible breath, not quite a sigh. He sat in the captain's chair and looked at the crew around him. "Let's go catch us a fish," he said as the submarine roared into life and the dual turbines drove the three-hundred and sixty-foot-long submarine beneath the surface of the North Pacific, where a cold-blooded monster lay in wait.

Leaving Pearl Harbor behind it, and heading back out the way it had come, the *USS Mississippi* cut a slow path through the waters. It moved at a leisurely fifteen knots, travelling not in a straight line but rather circling, baiting the shark to come after it.

The communication line through the sonar room was open, and Captain Lewis was in constant contact with the radioman. He wanted to know the minute anything was picked up. The *Charlotte* had already spoke about how fast the creature had turned on them. Rising from nowhere, to crash against the front end of the craft, taking out their sonar array and sphere.

"Captain, we have something on radar. It's small, but coming in fast." The voice of Jose Del Rio, the Radioman of the Watch, came through the speakers.

"Is it the shark?" Lewis asked.

"I don't know, sir. The readings would suggest not. The size is too small to be the target, but it is heading right for us," Del Rio spoke. "Closing in at a rate of eighteen knots."

Captain Lewis did not wait to hear any more. He was out of his chair and calling down to the engine room. "Increase our speed to twenty knots. Hold the current course." He gave the order and turned to Woods. "Let's see if we can't tire this thing out a little first."

"Captain, we have two more targets." Del Rio's voice was panicked. "One is right underneath us. Brace for impact."

The words came, and Lewis called out the order to all those in his immediate vicinity, but it was too late. Something crashed against the underside of the submarine and sent people flying in all directions. The impact shook the entire submarine, and as bodies landed in twisted piles on the floor, an alarm began to sound.

"I need a status report, now!" Lewis called through one channel. "Change our course by fifteen degrees, increase speed to twenty-two knots," he called down to the throttleman.

"Captain, we lost them," Del Rio spoke, and then immediately followed up with a fresh update. "Two more coming in up ahead of us. Eighteen knots and closing."

"Take us down to the floor, now," Lewis called through to the engine room, ordering the planesman to take them even deeper. "They want to play, then we will play, but we set the rules." Lewis looked at Woods, who was dabbing at a nasty gash on his forehead. He had broken his fall with his face, but would not let it interfere with his duties.

"Yes, sir." Woods nodded, acting without hesitation. He moved from the radio to the torpedo room. "Load the torpedo tubes. I want two Mark 60's in the water now," he ordered.

"Also, I need a medic to report to the control room immediately," Lewis ordered, nodding at his XO.

The wheels were set in motion, and before long, the submarine shook as the MK60 CAPTOR mines were deployed in the water behind them.

The status reports came back that the impact with the shark had resulted in some minor damage to the submarine's hull, but nothing would cause it any real problems.

"Sir," Maloney called out. "I've got the *Bremerton* here. They have also picked up two targets coming from the south."

"I thought there was only one of these fuckers," Captain Lewis growled at his XO.

"That was the intel we received, sir," Woods answered.

"Then get me the admiral on the line, because they need to know what's going on down here." Lewis dropped into his chair and waited for the admiral to join them.

CHAPTER 12

Martin sat in the admiral's quarters and listened to the message that was relayed to them. There were multiple sharks attacking the submarines.

"She's bred," Martin whispered, but his words were enough to bring all eyes onto him. "It can't be."

"Care to elaborate for us, Doctor?" the admiral asked.

"It can't be possible. A shark, the great white for example, doesn't reach sexual maturity until they are fifteen. Even then they only have single young at any one time. But it sounds as if my Megalodon has bred. Those are her children out there." Martin looked around the room at the gathered faces.

"So there are more things like her out there?" The tension in the room grew.

"I don't know. I mean, she had to come from somewhere. That was never explained to me. But, she can't have had that many young so fast. That would mean there are at least five, plus her. Her biology is changing too much, too fast." Martin began to stumble over his words as his mind began to run in a different directions, thinking of the possible implications of the tests he had run all those years ago.

"Are you telling us that we might be facing more than one of these supersharks out there?" Admiral Walters stared at Martin.

"I don't know," he admitted.

"What do you mean?" Walters' face darkened. The spacious room on the aircraft carrier quickly became an airless vacuum, the walls closed in and offered no chance of escape.

He opened his mouth to speak, but Marcus stepped up, physically moving between the Admiral and the scientist.

"I think what Dr. Lucas is trying to say is that five years ago, he worked on a project that was not finished and never tested in any situation beyond the confines of the laboratory. He cannot say with any degree of certainty what has happened in the intervening period, as he has had no direct involvement with the creature." Marcus spoke smoothly, the words coming naturally to him. The admiral, while clearly still enraged, was left with no choice but to back down.

"Nature is a funny thing. If we mess with it, there is no telling what may happen if we lose control of the situation," Martin added, his composure returned.

"Now is not the time to get cryptic on me, Dr. Lucas. I do not like the way this conversation is going. You had better hope that these are the only creatures we come up against. You don't want me to start thinking you may have been working against us these last five years also," the admiral growled. A vein had started to bulge in the side of his neck, adding to the angry image that he presented.

"I'm not being cryptic, but don't you see it? It all makes sense. That, out there, Omega-Base-Six. That is where she was born, the version of her that she truly is. It was her home, her territory," Martin raised his voice and did not care who he was talking to, rank was irrelevant as far as he was concerned.

Marcus made a motion for him to calm down, but Martin shook it off.

"We have covered that already Dr. Lucas and—"

Martin didn't give the admiral time to finish speaking, cutting him off mid-sentence. "No, you don't understand. That is her home. It is where she is raising her young."

A heady silence swept around the room, as the words began to sink in. Some heads digesting the information quicker than others.

"She attacked the *Chosin* because it threatened her family. Her home was in danger. When we were on the base, it responded to Corporal Gunn jumping down to help me. When he died, I was angry and kicked at the computer terminal. She registered it as a threat and attacked, just as nature had always intended her to do. Don't you see?" Martin asked, hoping one of the group would put it together.

"If we kill her young, she will see the submarine group as a threat, and she will eliminate them," Admiral Walters spoke, nodding his head as he talked.

"Exactly, possibly even the whole base. Now, I don't believe she would sink a carrier like this, but I see plenty of other ships and vessels out in the water that would not stand a chance if she decided to attack. You don't know this bitch like I do, sir." Martin stared at the admiral.

"Shit on a fucking shovel," the admiral snarled as he snatched up the phone. The line did not have time to connect before the explosion rumbled through the room like thunder.

CHAPTER 13

"We got them," Del Rio's voice came through the communicator. There was a small round of cheers as the good news travelled through the sub.

The mine detonated, and while the sub rocked in response to the explosion, it was designed to keep cutting a smooth path through the water.

"Stay alert, there are two more out there, at least," Captain Lewis spoke above the cheers.

The jubilant celebrations fell quiet and they realized that even though their enemy was something unlike anything they had ever faced before, it was precisely that which made it so dangerous. Having been out on a training exercise, none of the people on-board any of the submarines in their small group had any idea what was going on. Not until something attacked and disabled the *Charlotte* and a random message was received about a crazy shark. Only once they had taken the first blow did Captain Lewis realize the threat was to be taken seriously.

"Captain," Del Rio's voice whispered in Lewis's ear.

"Go ahead," Lewis instructed, hearing the trepidation in the man's voice.

"They are still coming." Not trepidation, but disbelief. That was what the words were coated in.

"You mean the other two?" Lewis confirmed, pushing his radioman for specifics.

"Those too, sir." There was something in the man's voice, something else, buried beneath the suspended belief.

"What wrong, Del Rio?" Lewis pushed, his own voice turning harsh.

"It's the big one, the shark... she is ... I've never seen anything like it. She is closing in at twenty-five knots from one thousand yards and closing, bearing three-zero degrees, north east." Del Rio focused himself, he grounded himself in his training, in his role as radioman.

Captain Lewis wasted no time; he dropped one channel and opened the other. "Incoming, three zero degrees, fire the 48's now."

"Captain," Gavin Woods called out, "we have two more coming in from starboard."

Panic began to fill the control room.

"Bring us closer to the surface, and increase speed to thirty knots," Lewis ordered down to the engine room, but it was not enough. The first shark hit from the starboard side, connecting with the hull by the reactor compartment. The shark bounced from the hull, its speed too much for the weight of its body. The blow was enough to shake the submarine, just at the time the torpedoes were fired. The change in pitch of their launch was all the time it took for the next two sharks to hit the submarine, pummelling the underside, damaging the torpedo tubes and perforating the hull.

Alarm bells started ringing throughout the sub. Doors sealed automatically as the water began to pour into the chamber.

"Bring us to the surface," Lewis called out, as he steadied himself.

The submarine was a hive of activity, people ran through the corridors, everybody who was not on an active shift jumped into action, not thinking, running on the pure instinct.

"Sir, the shark, she is closing in on us fast, five hundred meters," the voice called out above the wailing siren.

"Take us up, now, thirty-five knots," Lewis called.

The submarine responded almost immediately, rising to the surface at a steep angle and a fast pace. "We're moving too fast," a voice called out in the panic.

"Captain ..." Del Rio's warning came, but it was too late. The outcome was set, and nothing they did would change it.

The giant shark charged the rising submarine, passing just beneath the vessel. Its dorsal fin catching the rear of the craft, smashing the rudder as it sped past.

"Sir, she's passed beneath us, heading away at twenty-three knots," Del Rio called.

"Fire, two," Lewis ordered, looking around the room at the men who were once again picking themselves up from the floor.

Gavin Woods was one of them. He turned to look at Lewis as the port side torpedoes fired. His face was painted red. The wound on his scalp dishing out a profuse crimson tide of blood.

A few seconds later, the sound of the explosion hit the craft. The shock waves from the blast pushing the already fragile submarine around like a ragdoll beneath the waves.

"Did we hit the son of a bitch?" Lewis called through to Del Rio. For a few moments, there was no answer.

"We got something, sir," Del Rio answered.

"Something?"

"One of the smaller ones, I think. The big beast turned at the last second," Del Rio answered, his voice once again giving himself away.

"Where is she?" Lewis asked, knowing the answer already.

Lewis looked at the faces in the room, he looked around the bridge at the submarine that had been his for so long. "It's been a pleasure serving with you all," he spoke just moments before the impact.

The shark came powering up from beneath them and ploughed straight through the vessel. The submarine creaked and groaned, shaking until the moment she was shorn in half. Lewis stared as the creature passed through his boat.

Sea water flooded the sub, and people screamed. The lights went out and there was nothing but black. Lewis was surprised at how calm everything seemed to be, and how cold the water was.

The shark broke the surface and leaped into the air, twisting its body to crash back down into the water, pushing the two halves of the sub back down to the ocean floor.

CHAPTER 14

The battle unfolded within the line of site of the stricken *USS Charlotte*. The submarine had been told to limp home. They were damaged, and it was lucky they were still standing. The shark that had hit them was smaller than the mother.

"Captain, the *Mississippi,* she is gone, sir." The second-in-command relayed everything to the ship's captain, Duke Wynn.

"Gone?" Wynn exclaimed.

"As in that fucking shark just took them down, gone," Wynn's XO, Petty Officer Sandro Cruz, called out.

"Do we have a visual?" Wynn asked, his blood seething. At forty-five years of age, Wynn was the oldest submarine captain in the SUBRON 1 group. A career military man, who came from a family with a military career that he had traced back to the war of independence. Every generation served their country. Many had died for it, and Wynn would do the same in a second.

"Not anymore, sir. We had a breach but not the creature; I can´t find her anywhere," Cruz replied.

Captain Wynn strode through the command room and over to the sonar technician of the watch. "What do we have?" he asked the nervous young man. Riccardo Fonte was on his first assignment on a submarine. He was still shaken by the news of the attack, and now hearing talk of a submarine actually being sunk had him all flustered.

"I don't know, sir, I can't seem to … I don't know if … I have something. Moving in from the north-west. Two thousand yards and closing. Speed fifteen knots," the young man stuttered, his hands trembling as they sat on the display.

"Good job, Mr. Fonte." Wynn placed a hand on the younger man's shoulder. He understood that the man was afraid. They all were. Giving it a reassuring squeeze, Wynn moved away.

"This is the captain, load the torpedoes. I want this thing blown out of the water, now," Wynn spoke, and then moved back to the display screen offered by the cable fibre-linked periscope system.

The view was adjusted and the sub shuddered as the torpedoes were launched. The screens traced their passage through the water as they sped towards their target.

The large shark was gaining ground fast, its tall dorsal fin slicing through the water like a steel grey sail of a boat rising from the depths to claim a fresh batch of souls.

"Sir," Fonte called out. "There are two more targets closing in."

"Where?" Wynn asked, but he saw their fins on either side of the periscope image. The tracks of the torpedoes in the water changed, as their course switched to the new, closer threat.

"I need more fish out there," Wynn called, and the order to fire reverberated around the sub.

The first two explosions came almost simultaneously. The water erupting in a ball of water, steam, blood and flesh. The sharks were blown apart. They never stood a chance. Their immature bodies no match for the fifteen-hundred kilogram motorized explosives that slammed into their flanks. Even with the toughened skin passed down through engineered genetics, there was nothing the young sharks could do.

The mother on the other hand was a different story.

"Torpedoes away, sir," the voice came back to him. Captain Wynn was silent, his eyes fixed on the screen.

There was an eerie silence around the command room, for everybody understood what was at stake. The shark, through reasons that were far above their paygrade, had taken out a fully operation nuclear submarine in the *Mississippi*, and now the beast had turned her attentions on the *Charlotte*, a stricken ship, not much more than a sitting duck, ready and waiting for something to come along and wipe it out.

The two torpedoes surged towards the shark, whose fin disappeared beneath the surface of the water.

"She's going under, sir." Feedback came from all sides as everybody who could possibly sit behind machines and terminals monitored for anything and everything.

"The 48s are locked on, it doesn't matter," Captain Wynn answered them.

"Sir, she's accelerating, travelling twenty knots, twenty-two knots, and rising," Fonte spoke, his voice shaking as he realized what was happening. "She's heading straight for us."

"Increase our speed, whatever you can get out of the engines, get it," Wynn called down to the engine room.

The shark leaped from the water, rising up from the waves just ahead of the speeding torpedoes. The gargantuan body shot clear of the ocean and came crashing down again, not slamming the surface, but diving into it head first.

"Did you see that?" Cruz asked his captain and mentor.

"Did you expect me to miss it?" Wynn answered, not able to break his gaze on the water.

The shark was a twisted image of a living thing. The body was enormous, more in line with a whale. Her elongated head and upward tilting nose had the effect of pulling back the flesh around the beast's mouth, giving her a permanent grimace of anger and hate.

"Sir, it cleared the fish. They are coming around but it is closing fast," Fonte spoke quicker and quicker.

"Everybody brace yourselves," Wynn roared. "We need evasive action, now. Push this thing to the limit!"

"Captain," Fonte called out, unable to contain himself.

The first impact was a dull thud, which made the entire submarine shudder. The craft was shunted to one side so hard that everybody fell in a tangle of limbs. The sharp, crisp sound of snapping bones was audible. Cries of pain echoed around the craft.

Wynn and his officers fell to the floor of the command room. People cried out as limbs and flesh collided with one another and with the litany of consoles and machines. Wynn cried out as his leg snapped above the knee as his XO fell against him.

"What was that?" Cruz asked as he tried to get to his feet.

There was no time for answers. The first of the two torpedoes hit. The warhead collided with the already-damaged rear of the craft, destroying the rudder, the propellers and the ballast tanks. Metal twisted and tore as the explosion ripped through the craft. The propeller and shafts disappeared in a billowing cloud of grey smoke. Shards of metal and twisted pieces of propeller rained down on the submarine which was listed at a severe angle as it began to sink.

There was no time to react. No chance for a final goodbye or a last stand, for the second torpedo hit in the middle of the craft, decimating the berthing area, sending a fireball shooting through the tube, ripping through everything that stood in its way. The command post, located on the second level, shook and tore apart. The sound of the explosion rumbled like thunder, and the screams of those around him as they burned were the final things Duke Wynn heard before his life was snuffed out.

The submarine exploded, and fire consumed everything, before the North Pacific claimed its second prize.

CHAPTER 15

The news of the *Mississippi's* demise was filtering back through to those back at Pearl Harbor, just as the *Charlotte* was preparing to launch her torpedoes at the charging beast. The tension in the room was thick enough that not even a knife would be sufficient to cut it. A chainsaw maybe.

"This isn't going very well," Marcus whispered to Martin. They stood by the windows, looking out to sea. Their gaze was not scanning for signs of the conflict, but rather fixated on the distant spec that was Omega-Base-Six.

"They killed her babies," Martin answered dryly. "She will make them pay,"

"What would you have them do?" Director Cove had joined the two men. While between them, the rank and file was still in place, the grand scheme of things had developed to a point where they were no more than simple bystanders. People were playing games with paygrades so far above theirs, the numbers were not even distantly related.

"I still say the same. We need to lure her back home, and bury her in it. She is too fast and too strong to be shot down. She is smart, and not because I made her that way. The shark itself is from a different time, a time where it was kill or be killed, and that sort of intelligence just doesn't exist anymore. Not for us." Martin looked at the two men.

"What do you mean?"

"I mean for us, the good guys, the world is full of choices and options. But what about the Middle East, the terrorists? They sweep through the world. They wage war and they conquer. Kill or be killed." Martin worked hard to make sure his voice was a whisper.

"It got the *Charlotte*, too," an announcement was made, and the clamour and chatter among the various ranks of high-grade military officials increased.

The number of people in the room had swollen to the point where it became uncomfortable, but nobody showed any signs of leaving. Decisions needed to be made, and war was fought in luxuriously decorated offices, and not out on the battlefield.

"Fuck it," Martin said slamming a balled left fist into his open right hand. He moved away from his companions and pushed through the throng of military personnel.

"Martin," Marcus called after him, but his plea fell on deaf ears.

"Admiral," Martin tried to interrupt the conversation between the admiral and another military figure whose chest seemed to be decorated with all manner of pins and ribbons.

Martin was ignored.

"Admiral," he spoke firmly and moved between the two men, cutting off their conversation. "If you want to end this, then you better damn well listen to me," Martin spoke before the older man had a chance to give voice to the rage his eyes expressed.

"This had better be good."

"You need to send explosives out to Omega-Base-Six, you need to prime that thing to blow. We have killed her young, she will not stop. We have her engaged at the moment. Tell that submarine to run, pull her away as far as they can. We fill that base with enough warheads to sink a continent, and get me close enough to activate the chip and bring her home." Martin didn't just suggest, he advised, his words not a question or a suggestion for the admiral to follow, but an order. He spoke with confidence and stared down the military senior.

"Are you suggesting we use our own people as bait, son?" the second military man spoke up.

"I'm suggesting we kill this fucking bitch before we lose her. What happens if she leaves? We kill her young, she takes out your subs and then what. She escapes. What damage are we willing to risk she causes out there?" Martin did not give them time to even ponder his questions, let alone answer them before he continued. "We have her cornered now, it is our chance. I say we distract her, just long enough to get everything set up."

The whole room had stopped their individual chattering and turned their attention to the conversation that was playing out in the corner of the room.

"You make the call, Admiral," the older man said.

Admiral Walters once again glowered at Martin, the look of contempt that he had borne before was nothing in comparison to the look of utter disdain that filled his eyes now.

"Tell the *Bremerton* to head back out, make sure that damned creature follows them." The order was given to the room, and the rush to pass them on began. "You had better be right about this. Otherwise, every death out there today will be your fucking problem," he growled at Martin before turning and storming away.

"You got balls as big as my mistress's tits," the older man said to Martin with a laugh.

"Thank you, sir," Martin replied.

"Let's take a walk," the older man said.

Martin opened his mouth to raise an issue, but the old man cut him off. "Don't worry, son, nobody questions my judgement around here."

He held his hand out for Martin. "Commandant Lawrence Abbott."

Martin took the man's hand. "Doctor—"

"I know who you are, Dr. Lucas," the commandant said with a smile. "Let's take a walk and talk about your future, shall we?"

CHAPTER 16

Everything had happened so fast, the crew of the *Bremerton* had not had time to process the situation. They were at war. That was the mind-set that had settled. Regardless of the enemy, they were under attack and that warranted only one response.

When they saw the *Mississippi* fire her torpedoes, they had been thrown onto a path that none of them had any control over. When the *Charlotte* was lost, their rage was given a direction. So when the order finally came to turn the sub around and head out to sea, the move was greeted with a cheer.

"We are gonna teach this bitch a lesson," Captain Mark Norris spoke to his crew. "Take us down to one hundred and fifty feet. Set speed at twenty knots."

The orders were filtered through and everybody on watch busied themselves with their tasks. They were all aware that the final juvenile shark was out there, but the mother shark was the creature they were most interested in.

The torpedo tubes were loaded with MK60 mines. They had received orders to drop the first two mines at five-hundred yard intervals.

"I want to know the second anything comes within range," Norris said to his sonar technician.

"Yes, sir," the man answered, his eyes glued to the screens before him.

A silence settled over everybody as they immersed themselves in their tasks. It was an easier feat than they expected, to cast aside the knowledge that a hundred-ton monster was hunting them.

"How far do you need to lead her?" Benjamin Collins, the subs XO asked.

"As far as is needed," Norris replied. "As far as is needed."

"Why don't we just plant some more mines and be done with it?" someone suggested.

"She is too smart, too fast," Norris answered, even though the question had not been aimed at him in person. "We are to lead the shark out to sea and make sure, that when the word comes in, we turn her around and bring her to shore. Those are our orders, and we will stick to them," Captain Norris addressed his crew.

"Captain, the first mine is ready to be deployed," the quartermaster of the watch reported.

"Very good," the captain said as he braced himself.

The *Bremerton* was an older sub, the oldest in the current SUBRON 1 group, and as such at times needed to be treated gentle, like any older lady should. However, the time for gentle graces was over. With a rumble, the first mine was ejected into the ocean behind them.

"Take us down to two-five hundred feet," Norris ordered.

The submarine sank to its new depth and settled, the speed constant.

"Captain, the second mine is all clear for launch," the weapons officer confirmed.

"Proceed," Captain Norris said, as he once again braced himself.

"Maybe we should circle back, Captain, get her attention again," Collins asked.

"No, that won't be necessary. She's out there. I know it," Norris whispered his response.

Not five seconds later, in a series of near simultaneous occurrences, one of the two mines activated, spilling their torpedo cargo into the water. Oliver Howard, the sonar technician on watch, spoke up to announce that they had something on radar, and the torpedo exploded, having found its target.

The final juvenile shark exploded in a mess of flesh and gone, the toughened skin no match for the detonating warhead. The ocean turned murky with blood and chunks of shark meat. Through it appeared the hulking figure of the Megalodon. The ocean was heavy with the meaty taste of blood, and the beast that had taken the lives of her children was close at hand. The beast sank down low, and waited for the right time to strike.

***

On the docks of Pearl Harbor, the *USS Port Royal* was being loaded with explosives and the crew gathered. The ship had the capabilities for a crew of over three hundred and fifty, but there was no need for such numbers, and so the shift was deemed ready to depart with a contingency of thirty-six men, and four women. Including Dr. Martin Lucas and Special Agent in Charge Marcus Lovell.

"So what did the old man want with you?" Marcus asked, taking Martin by the arm and leading him away from the always prying ears.

"Nothing special. He just wanted to talk about my plans, offered me a job on the base working in their biometrics division," Martin answered.

"They have a biometrics division here?" Marcus was confused. It was his understanding that all of the biological-grade military science programs were located in a locked-down facility in the heart of Washington.

"They will if I say yes to the job." Martin smiled.

"Very nice." Marcus nodded.

"Yes, but we just need to survive this mission first," Martin said. "Now if you excuse me, I need to go set this control unit into the computer system on board and see if I can get it working."

"Wait a minute, you don't even know if it is going to work?" Marcus all but cried out.

"Of course not. I mean, this baby has been sitting here on a lost military base for years and has gone through several rough patches in the last few hours alone. There is no way I can guarantee that anything will work at all." Martin gave Marcus a wink and walked away.

"Oh, fan-fucking-tastic." The agent sat back against the guardrail of a frigate.

Martin made this way up into the ship's combat information center and positioned himself behind one of the large computer terminals. He pulled his control unit from the inside pocket of his jacket and got to work hooking it up to the computer.

The matter was complicated enough by the fact that the computers had advanced somewhat since Martin's unit had existed, and he was going to have to work around getting it hooked up to the machine.

With everything set, Martin got to work, noting down the different frequencies as he went through them all until he found the channel that allowed him to connect with the creature, and at least override its basic brain function long enough to redirect its attention towards the Omega-Base-Six structure.

The closer the shark was to the control unit, the more powerful the signal would be. In theory. Martin had never put that to the test, and had no way of guaranteeing the chip would even still have an impact on the shark.

"All set, Doc? You're the star of this show." The *Port Royal's* captain, Mark Hughes, placed a hand on Martin's shoulder.

"Yes, sir. Just got to get into position and fire this baby up," Martin answered, his eyes focused on the equipment before him.

He didn't want to look at the captain directly, for he was afraid the man would see the truth buried in his eyes. Martin was struggling with being back on a ship. Surrounded by military personnel. His mind would not shut out the echo of gunfire. His every thought and movement creaked and groaned with the faded, but never gone, screams of the dying.

Martin sat back and closed his eyes. As crazy as everything was, the only thing he could force his mind to focus on at that point in time, was a drink.

Not a drink to be the first of one, then five then ten until a black-out washed him away into a few hours of silence, but a single drink, to calm his nerves and ease his shaking hand.

"We will get you into position, Doctor, don't you worry about that. The explosives are being loaded onto a bird as we speak. Once we reach the base, they will fly out and get everything ready. You work your magic, we blow that fucker back to hell and get back home for a cold beer and game of football," Hughes said with a smile. He was an older man with a shock of black hair and a thick black beard, and in between the two expanses of black, shone two eyes of a brilliant blue. A cold blue, which gave the man a steely glaze. As the man walked away, Martin decided he would not want to see the captain if he was angry.

The cruiser set sail and pulled away from Pearl Harbor. It was a three-hour journey to the base, in which time the *Bremerton* had taken out the final young, and the end game was approaching.

"I hope this works," Marcus whispered as he crouched down beside Martin.

"You and me both."

CHAPTER 17

The *Bremerton* reduced her speed and headed for the surface. There had been no sign of the shark, and Captain Norris was starting to get nervous. They should have at least seen it following them by now. If the shark had turned around and was heading back to the base then everything was lost.

As he surveyed the ocean surface, his eyes long since accustomed to spotting things on the undulating horizon, Norris held his breath.

He saw something, in the distance. It was not more than a spec and quickly slipped beneath the waves as if knowing it had been spotted.

As if on cue, the sonar picked up a reading from the same location. "Captain, we've found her," Eric Matthews spoke, spinning around to face the bridge.

"No, she's found us," the captain corrected.

"She's coming in at twenty knots, sir," Matthews relayed the data.

"Increase our speed to twenty-three knots. I want to keep ahead of her, and I know she has more gas in her than that." Norris turned away from the screens and took his seat. "Take us down to one hundred feet. I want two more mines laid in the water at five-hundred-yard intervals again." He gave the instructions to those that needed to hear them.

The submarine sank back beneath the surface of the North Pacific, and a distance behind them, the shark did the same.

"First mine has been deployed, sir," the weapons officer advised a few moments later.

"Good, hold our current course. I want to know this creature's speed, its direction, everything. Even if nothing changes, I want to know."

***

The *Port Royal* made smooth work of the trip to the base, and by the time they had come alongside the hulking structure, which even now, listing as it was, dwarfed the cruiser, making it look like a matchbox model.

"Sir, the *Bremerton* has the shark on her tail. They are leading it out and awaiting further command." The words were relayed from the radar room through to the ships XO, Gemma Brown, a green-eyed, painfully attractive woman, who came with a warning label, at least, the other techs on board the boat had warned Martin about her.

She was as dangerous as she was beautiful, and second to none when it comes to two things, giving someone a verbal beat down, and milking a cock. The second was admittedly more conjecture than based on any factual knowledge, but Martin was not willing to argue on either front.

"That's good news. But even so, I want people on the .50 calibre guns, and get the Phalanx online too. I'm not taking any chances with this one. This bitch took down the *Chosin* a few days ago, and we will not even entertain the idea of a similar fate." Captain Hughes looked around at his crew as he spoke.

They were running on bare bones, but they would have to make do. It was not a long and protracted skirmish that lay ahead of them, but a short wild ride, and he had full confidence that his crew were more than capable of dealing with it.

"Sir, the choppers are ready with the explosives." Brown relayed the information she had received from the command room back at the Harbor.

"Send them out," Hughes confirmed. "Now we wait, ladies and gentlemen, now we wait."

The *Port Royal* made a wide loop and circled the base, keeping their eyes on the ocean, and their ears pricked for any sign or warning from the *Bremerton*. None came.

"Get me in touch with the sub," Hughes ordered after they had not received any update from the old submarine.

"I'm trying sir, but she's not responding," the worried-sounding voice of a radar technician came back from the radar room.

"What do you mean she is not responding?" Hughes was out of his seat and striding towards the radioman who had delivered the bad news.

The man did not flinch when the captain appeared beside him. "I've been trying to reach them for five minutes, but there has been no response. Nothing, not even static. The *Bremerton* just isn't there anymore."

The words hung in the air. If the *Bremerton* was lost, then they were screwed on several levels. Besides the fact that the shark had taken out three nuclear submarines, the larger concern was they had no idea where the hell the beast was.

"I want everybody alert. Keep hailing the sub, if they don't respond, we will have to head out and look for them." Hughes relayed his orders and began to pace around the command room.

The ocean stretched out before him, the sky a cloudless blue, the ocean a steely shade of the same colour. They were just making their third pass around the base when the helicopters came overhead. They landed one by one on the rear of the cruiser. It was deemed that the safest way to bring the explosive on board the base was from the cruiser itself.

They would tie up against the station unloading the charges on three of the six sides. The crew would set and prime everything and be extracted by the choppers from what remained of the decimated helipad.

That changed, however, when communication with the sub was lost.

Captain Hughes was on deck to greet the helicopter teams and their respective pilots.

"I'm afraid there has been a change of plans," Hughes began the conversation directly, for there was no time to be lost to formality.

"What's changed?" Chuck Dillashaw, the pilot of one of the two Seahawk helicopters, asked as he shook the captain's hand.

"We lost contact with the *Bremerton* about ten minutes ago." The captain and the pilot walked away together.

"Want me to take a look? I can unload my supplies and be out there to recon in twenty minutes," the pilot spoke, understanding the seriousness of the issue.

"I'd appreciate that. We will drop off the supplies at a single point of contact and head out. If needed, we will intercept the creature and keep her busy ourselves until the explosives are ready and the base is empty." Hughes and the pilot descended into a short conversation, and with a handshake and a salute, the rules of their engagement were changed.

The *Port Royal* made one final loop around the base, coming up alongside the armoury wing of the structure. The crew got to work moving everything into the structure, the entire shipment of explosives were offloaded and the necessary hands were also helped aboard. It would be up to them to set the charges and call the second Seahawk to rescue them.

"Captain, requesting permission to board the base and assist with laying the charges, sir," Marcus approached the captain the moment he returned to the command room.

"Request granted, Agent Lovell. I appreciate the assistance. You are familiar with the layout of the base. It would be an asset having you on board."

"It will be a pleasure, sir." Marcus saluted the captain and turned away.

Martin was standing waiting for him. His face was a picture of confusion.

"What are you doing?" he asked, disbelieving of what he had just heard.

"I'm doing my job. You need to do this, and I need to do that. Your history is with the shark, mine is with that base," Marcus began.

"I created the beast, that is on me. I'm the only one who can stop her," Martin countered, hoping above all other things he would be able to convince the man he already considered to be a friend to change his mind.

"I understand, I do. But that place took everything from me. I lost my husband, I lost my face, and my body. I don´t even have a fucking career to head back to. If anybody is going to be out there and ensure that that evil motherfucking place dies, then it has to be me." Marcus was resolute.

"I understand," Martin said, nodding his head. "Just make sure you are gone by the time that place blows."

"Don´t you worry about that. I will be long gone," Marcus replied.

CHAPTER 18

Chuck Dillashaw had been flying since before he was legally old enough to do so. He came from a family of pilots. Joining the military as a pilot had been the only thing he had ever wanted to do.

Yet as he took off from the deck of the *Port Royal,* it was with a heavy heart. It was the first flight that he did not look forward to. If the submarine had gone silent, then it only meant one thing.

He had flown in and out of hot zones during his career and had transported more broken and bleeding bodies than he cared to count, and left more than a few dead ones behind, but there was something different this time. It was too close to home. It was against an enemy that made no sense to him.

"What the hell is happening?" Tony Stewart, his co-pilot, asked as they dipped the nose of their bird just a little and headed out to sea.

"I have no idea, man. I'm just hoping we find them out there and that everything is just some mechanical fault somewhere." It was wishful thinking, but he was indulging himself, just this once. His helicopter was armed with four AGM-114 Hellfire missiles, and a GAU-16 .50 calibre machine gun. If needs must, he would use everything if it meant taking down the shark.

The Seahawk moved low over the surface of the ocean, and when they reached the area that they believed should contain the submarine, they found nothing. There was no sign of the ship, but that in itself did not prove anything. When a craft can survive underwater, not seeing it on the surface did not necessarily mean it had sunk in the more conventional term of the word.

"I don't see anything, and the *Port Royal* is also getting nothing but silence from them," Tony said as he craned his neck looking around for anything that might give some indication as to what had happened.

"I've got a bad feeling about this," Chuck muttered under his breath as he swung his bird around in a wide arc.

"Wait, what's that?" Tony pointed to the horizon. Nothing was immediately visible. Only when the roll of the ocean hit a downward trajectory did his sharp eyes catch it. A momentary flash of red, which only meant one thing.

"*Port Royal,* this is Dillashaw on Hawk-one-nine, do you read?" Chuck turned the helicopter towards the red spot, which had once again disappeared from view.

"Go ahead, Hawk," the *Port Royal* replied.

"We've got someone in a survival suit out here. We're taking a closer look, but it doesn't look good." Chuck shuddered at speaking the words and was reminded of the strange and heavy feeling he had when back on the cruiser.

"Roger that, Hawk, stay in contact, and stay alert," the *Port Royal* radioman replied, his words professional, but his tone was strained.

There were only a few minutes away from the location where they had seen the suit, only now, there was no sign of the thing. The surface was the water rolling with the gentle waves, and further out, the force of the Seahawk's large rotors caused a secondary disturbance, but for the rest, there was no sign of anything.

"I didn't imagine it," Tony said as they looked around for the red suit.

"I know, I saw it too," Chuck replied.

He took the chopper closer to the water, the disturbance from the power motors causing the sea to swell in a new perfect circle around the same diameter as the rotor span.

"What are you doing?" Tony asked, looking at the pilot.

"Just taking a closer look," Chuck said with a smile. "There!" he nearly shouted and thrust his finger ahead of them. A few hundred meters away another red figure bobbed on the water.

"Get the winch ready," Chuck ordered, but Tony was already out of his seat and moving to the back.

"You will have to get us closer to the water," Tony spoke, regretting his words before he had finished speaking them, but the truth was, there really was no other way.

The winch lowered, and so did the chopper. The red survival suits were designed to keep people alive. Rank was unimportant, making identification impossible until they were all in the chopper and safe. It made no difference, and a survivor was a survivor.

The blast from the rotors kicked up a misty wall of water and the swimmer had to cover his face with his hands until the worst of it was over. When he looked up again, the winch was close enough for him to grab a hold of. Without waiting to ensure he was truly secure in the harness, he gave the signal and the rescue cable began to rise.

For a short time, everything seemed to freeze. Time stopped for both for the man in the ocean and the pair in the chopper. Slowly, the man rose into the air, holding on for dear life as he slipped further and further out of the roughly fastened straps.

"Hurry up," Tony called through to Chuck.

"He's not secure," Chuck called back.

The pilot held the chopper while staring out of the side window of the helicopter at the struggling figure that dangled below.

"I know, but there's something under him," the co-pilot shouted back as the enormous shadow grew beneath the surface.

Chuck saw what Tony was talking about, but had no time to react. The shadow rose, not gaining true form until it left the water.

A grey snout, the jaws opening, wider than a man is tall, row after row of enormous serrated teeth, each one a cutting, shearing, implement of total destruction. Several were missing from where the shark had undoubtedly bitten into the submarine. Blood smeared its mouth as its jaws stretched to the maximum and began to snap closed.

Chuck reacted fast, jerking the stick and throwing the chopper to the left, launching both the partially rescued submariner and the unprepared co-pilot.

Tony had the presence of mine to grab out, catching himself just before he fell from the other side of the copper. Beneath them, the submariner fell from the hoist. He flew through the air and landed in the ocean with a heavy and awkward splash. The shark twisted its body and crashed down lengthways against the water just before Tony let loose with a burst of fire from the mounted .50 calibre gun on the side of the Seahawk.

The bullets hit their target, but seemed to do no discernible damage. Blood clouded the water, the projectiles at least now finding a way through the upper layer of flesh, but the creature sank beneath the waves, seemingly unperturbed by the onslaught wrought down from above.

"Shit, we lost him," Tony growled.

"That bitch is still down there, and we are gonna call her out," Chuck answered as he spun the bird around and pushed the chopper ahead of the shark's projected path.

"I meant our package," Tony called out his correction. "But I like your thinking."

"Aw, you say the sweetest things," Chuck called back as he pushed the chopper to climb before buzzing down to the sea once more.

The rescue harness was still swinging beneath the chopper, the only thing Chuck could do was hover the thing over the man, who was still swimming against the tide. Behind him, the shark's fin rose as tall as a billboard.

Tony opened fire as soon as he saw the tall, grey appendage. Bullets ripped holes in the thinner section of the creature's body.

"She is going back under," he roared, angered at the shark's refusal to accept the authority of hot .50 calibre lead.

"Not if I can help it, hold on!" Chuck screeched above the drone of the machine gun. A few seconds later, a Hellfire air-to-surface missile was fired and cast a direct line towards the monster.

Chuck gave a cry of joy as he pulled the chopper around in a tight arc and swung the harness over the swimmer again.

Grabbing the harness for all he was worth, the man held on, as not one hundred yards behind him, the missile found its target on the once-again looming shark. The explosion shook the creature doing enough damage to break off the attack, but even Chuck saw the beast swam away under its own power.

"He's on, pull him up," Tony called. He had left the gun and was watching the slow and steady ascent of the stranded mariner.

There was no sign of the shark; but that said nothing. She was somewhere licking her wounds and readying itself for another strike.

"*Port Royal,* do you read?" Chuck called.

"Go ahead, Hawk," the voice came back.

"The *Bremerton* is gone. We've got one survivor on the winch. The shark is still out here, we've unloaded on her with .50 calibres, and some hellfire," Chuck relayed the basics of their encounter with the shark back to the cruiser.

"Roger that, Hawk. Can you confirm if the target is still a threat?" There was a faint glimmer of hope in the voice.

"I'm afraid so. She ate everything up and kept coming." Chuck couldn't believe what he was saying, and if he had not seen the creature take the hellfire hit and keep swimming, he would never thought it possible.

***

"Sir, the *Bremerton* is lost." The message from the pilots was passed through the cruiser to Captain Hughes.

He listened to the update and sat down, absorbing the information without reaction, allowing himself the time to think his response through.

Three submarines had been lost to the beast. Three crews who would never see their families again, and with nothing stopping the shark from heading out into open waters, they risked losing the beast for good.

He needed to take action, but action without thought would only add to the day's death toll. Calmer heads were needed, only they would prevail against a beast that defied nature.

Captain Hughes rose from his chair, and he looked everybody in the eye, his face giving away nothing, other than his clear, unmoving certainty, that they would not fail again.

"We have lost too many today," he began his address. "This cluster fuck ends now, with us. Power up the engines, we are going fishing," the captain ordered his crew and walked over to Martin, who sat with a grave face, his mouth set with a mixture of determination and insurmountable guilt.

"Dr. Lucas," he spoke calmly.

"Yes, sir?" Martin replied, swallowing hard.

"Be honest with me, how certain are you of your plan?" The captain's eyes bored into Martin, rooting around inside him, trying to find not the answer, but the reality behind the answer he was going to give.

"I would say seventy-five percent, sir." Martin's mouth was dry.

Captain Hughes mulled this over for a moment. "That will have to do then. We are heading after the shark, and when we get there, we will lead it back here. But I will need you to hold up to your end of the deal."

"I'll do my best, sir," Martin said, forcing his voice to sound resolute.

The captain walked away, and as the cruiser began to pick up a head of steam, Martin lost himself in his work.

He had never actually tried the chip. The whole thing had been experimental. However, he had based everything off a similar design that he had used in a new bio-suit allowed a sort of override to anybody that found themselves injured or lost in battle. Not exactly a remote control, but more a series of suggestions, which if delivered on a strong signal, would prompt said individual to follow a certain path. Either away from danger or back on the right track if they had somehow wandered off course.

CHAPTER 19

On the lower deck of Omega-Base-Six, the teams had formed and were working their way around the base in opposing rotations, the plan being for them to meet on the opposite side of the base and make their way up to the chopper for extraction.

Those plans seemed to change when the cruiser turned and left.

"The *Port Royal* is leaving," one of the crewmen called, standing at the dirty and cracked window.

He held a long stick of dynamite in his hands, while his assigned partner was drilling a hole into the main stanchions. The dynamite would be inserted into the whole and the detonator synced.

A third member of the group moved along and connected everything, linking the individual dynamite charges with a centralized detonator.

For the first team, that was Marcus, who had experience in explosives and happily volunteered for the task for the simple reason that he wanted something to do, he needed to play a real part in the base's destruction. His scarred hands and distorted fingers worked in a strangely nimble way as they danced around the delicate explosives.

He found peace in the work, and realized just how much he missed it, and how much sitting behind a desk waiting for the years to tick on through to retirement had gotten him down.

"Then we had better focus and get this done." Marcus looked up and answered the younger man, whose attention was fully focused on the departing cruiser.

"Right on, Agent," a grisly looking man with a thick handlebar moustache spoke up.

There had not been a chance for the team to be fully introduced, and Marcus had not taken on board all of the names that had been thrown at him. He believed the man was called Norman. He remembered, because he had snickered when the man was introduced, because he looked anything but a Norman.

"Jenkins, there's a hole here waiting, if you leave your wife gaping like this, some other bastard is going to plug her. Get your head in the game," the man growled, making the younger recruit jump.

"Yes, sir, Sergeant Major." He jumped to attention and re-joined their group.

The base was large, but with the urgency embedded in them from the knowledge of the lost submarines, the groups made relatively short work of the setup. Each team drilled a total of thirty-seven holes, each one packed with explosive charges.

By the time they were ready, each member of the re-combines group was soaked with sweat. The *Port Royal* had sailed away to nothing more than a dot in the distance.

"I'm going to do one more sweep and make sure everything is set, and then I will meet you all up on the roof," Marcus spoke to the sergeant major, who he refused to accept as being Norman anything.

"The chopper is on the way. Make sure you are back in time," the grizzled officer responded.

Marcus gave no answer, but turned and jogged down the corridor. There was no need for him to check the wiring. He knew everything was all expertly set, but he needed to feel that last rush. The final chance of sweeping a building, of being a real agent, not some paper monkey.

He slowed his pace as he rounded the corner. He didn't dawdle, that would have been foolish, but he wanted to savour it.

***

The Seahawk wobbled slightly as Chuck tried his best to hold his bird still. A wind was building out at sea, and the chopper was more than receptive to its change.

"Goddammit to hell and back again," Tony yelled from the body of the chopper.

"What's wrong?" Chuck asked, his attention was split between the instruments and the ocean. He could not take his mind from the fact that the creature was still out there, beneath them somewhere. Watching them.

"The damned winch is stuck, we need to pull him up," Tony said as he leaned over the side to grab at the rigging. "The cable too taut. We will have to get closer."

"No way," Chuck shot back.

"Then he's dead," Tony answered,

"If we go down any lower then we're dead. He'll just have to hold on," Chuck reasoned as he pulled the helicopter into a steep climb.

Beneath them, the water erupted once more. The shark launched itself, bypassed the suspended submariner, who himself was busy trying to scale the cord, and find himself in the relative sanctuary of the chopper. The shark was no longer interested in small prey. Its sights were set on the Seahawk. Its enormous body snapped at the tail, its jaws once again open and ready to clamp down and rip the flying iron apart.

Rounds from the cruiser's .98 calibre Mk 38 autocannon peppered the water, marching along until they found their target. The force of the rounds impact was enough to knock the shark back into the water. The large shells buried into its skin. Fired in accurate bursts, they tore a large hole in the beast's flank.

The shark crashed back down into the water with a sound that boomed above everything else. Chuck rose with the Seahawk, unable to prevent the poor man beneath them from swinging wild in the wind.

In the back of the bird, Tony was busy working on the winch. His version of working at least. He was kicking the unit with his heavy boots, and cursing in every language he knew. Which was six, unless you discredited cursing, for then the total would have been reduced to but one.

"It's working," he cried out, more in surprise than triumph.

The winch growled and Tony leaned further than he was comfortable to haul the man into the chopper. He was unconscious. He had only held on because his survival suit had been caught in the harness, preventing him from falling.

Yanking the man out of both the harness and the safety suit, Tony forgot about the shark and busied himself with checking their new passenger. The man was alive, and his pulse was strong. However, he was unresponsive to everything Tony tried. Deciding that the only thing to do was make him comfortable, as much as that was possible in the back of a military Seahawk that was not configured for search and rescue efforts.

"That was fucking close," he called through to Chuck, who was glad his back was to his co-pilot, for he was sure that his face was as pale as a corpse; no freshly dead thing either, but something that has had time to sit and the blood to settle.

"You sure took your time," Chuck called through to the *Port Royal.*

"You're welcome, Hawk," the *Port Royal* radioman replied. "Now get out of here, we are going to bring this bitch home."

"Roger that, good luck and God speed." With his orders received, Chuck took his bird up, eager to put the ocean as far below him he was able.

"How's he doing?" Chuck asked back to the Tony, who was still sitting beside their passenger.

"He's out, but I don't like his chances." Tony looked down at the man, who had grown even paler since he had been pulled onto the chopper.

"Hold on," Chuck spoke to the unknown man. "We'll get you some help."

CHAPTER 20

"If that didn't piss her off, I don't know what will." Captain Hughes had watched the horizon and saw the shark erupt from the water.

He was glad to have armed his ships guns as a precautionary measure, because without them, the helicopter would have been lost, and more bodies would have been added onto his conscience.

"Dr. Lucas, I believe now would be a good time for you to come to our aid." The captain walked over to Martin's console and stood behind him.

The presence was an additional pressure, but Martin was pretty sure he had reached the point whereby any such additions would not register. He was maxed out on pressure. His hands shook as his hands moved over the terminal, logging into the software that would allow him to access the chip.

"You have done this before, right?" a nervous technician asked.

"Of course," Martin answered. "With injured soldiers, guiding them to a medical unit, on a training exercise … in a simulator."

The collective inhalation at this news was almost audible.

"Well, I have faith in you, Doctor," Captain Hughes said in a bid to relieve some of the tension. "Do we have anything?" he asked the sonar technician.

"Um, yes, sir, she just appeared at five thousand yards, bearing three-zero degrees north, sir." The young man did not raise his head from the screens as he spoke.

"Doctor, how does that suit you?" Hughes asked, but Martin was ready for him.

"I am bringing the chip online now," Martin spoke as lights began to burn on the screen. "I will need to use suggestion, directional impulses," Martin spoke, but was more than anything thinking out loud.

"You leave that to us, you just keep that bitch under control," Hughes replied. "I want the Phalanx brought online. We are going to get this bitch's attention. The 38's too, I want us loud out there.

Make us look so good she can't resist." He strode across the command room to stare out to sea.

The boat cut a fast pace through the water, and Martin worked furiously to get the chip activated. Sweat blinded him as every attempt he made to bring the chip online failed.

On the deck of the *Port Royal*, the various gunmen sat in position, ready to unleash seven levels of hell on the beast, their fingers itching for the chance to fill it with lead and claim the kill as their own.

"Sir, the chip is online," Martin called, relief surging through him.

"Good news, Doctor." Hughes didn't turn around, but kept his eyes on the water. "Let's start making some noise."

"That won't be necessary, sir," the radarman spoke. "She is heading our way on the same course, moving twenty knots."

"Is that you, Doctor?" Hughes asked.

"No, the chip is active but my commands are failing," Martin answered.

"What do you mean failing?" the captain asked.

"There is something interfering with the program," Martin said, sweat peppering his brow as he concentrated. "If I didn't know any better I would say …"

"You would say what?" the captain asked when Martin failed to offer the answer freely.

"I would say that somebody else is out there with the same idea as me. My commands are being blocked." Martin looked up from behind his terminal.

"I was hoping you were going to say something else," the captain said solemnly.

"I'll keep working, there must be a way around, but you will need to buy me some time." Martin returned his gaze to the terminal.

"Open fire," the captain roared, not wanting to take any chances.

The guns roared as they emptied round after round into the water, following the bearings sent through. The water exploded as if caught in a violent storm.

"Three thousand yards and closing, sir."

"We've lost visual."

"She's going under." The voices came in a rush as everybody focused on the shark.

"Turn us around, take us back to Omega-Base-Six, and prepare to launch torpedoes, on my mark." Captain Hughes gave the instructions, reacting on instinct.

The cruiser was brought around in a sharp turn, and rocked as the two torpedoes were launched.

"The fish are clear, sir," the weapons officer reported back.

"Very good. Increase speed to thirty knots. I don't want to take any chances with this bitch." The captain began to pace around the command room. The torpedoes had not found their target, and that bothered him.

"One thousand yards, sir," the technician called as the boat began to finish her turn.

"Do we fire again, sir?"

"No, she's too close," Hughes called, his voice giving his emotions away.

"Sir, she's gone," the radar technician called out in surprise.

"Gone?" A strange silence swept over the room.

"She's beneath us," Martin realized and cried out.

"Brace, brace!" Hughes called.

"I've got control," Martin called, moments before the boat was rocked by an impact greater than an explosion.

The nine-thousand-ton vessel lurched violently to one side as the shark was diverted at the last minute by the impulse override from Martin's chip. The command room shook from the impact, and everybody was thrown to the floor. Screams rang out and sparks flew as computers shorted out.

There were no orders needed for the guns to resume their aquatic assault. Both cannons roared with anger as they unleashed their rage on the creature. Its muscular flank was peppered with lead, and blood filled the ocean. From close range, even the shark was not invulnerable.

"She's swimming around again, sir," a groggy voice called.

"Dr. Lucas," the captain called, his voice angry and short.

"The chip is active, sir. I managed to push him to one side, but the control is limited. We will need outrun her," Martin said, as he continued to adjust the settings.

"Get in touch with Omega-Base-Six, tell them we are coming in hot. They need to get out of there, now," Captain Hughes ordered.

The cruiser sped through the water, pushing all of thirty knots, and not far behind, the giant shark followed. Injured, broken and bleeding. She sank low to the ocean floor, her rage more than enough to carry her through.

CHAPTER 21

Marcus completed his lap of the base and reached the others just as the word came through from the *Port Royal*.

"Just in time. We need to get out of here now. There is a bird coming in hot. Look alive," the sergeant major instructed the men, who moved to the roof of the structure in the same two groups they had been in to rig the explosives.

The first group moved, taking the stairwell that, to their amazement, was still intact. The sound of the approaching chopper bounded through the stairwell. The first group was standing ready when the bird hovered low over the base's roof. As the first four men boarded the rescue chopper, the other team emerged into the room, with the sergeant major and Marcus holding back.

"What are you waiting for, Agent?" the sergeant major asked.

"Just taking a moment," Marcus laughed. "I know I'm being stupid—"

"Nah man, I know where you are, letting go of all of this, not an easy thing to do." The sergeant major stood beside Marcus and watched the approaching Cruiser.

The guns echoed as the craft drew closer. The substance behind their growls grew with each meter the distance between them was reduced.

Behind the cruiser was the shark, chasing them down like a hellhound unleashed from the unleashed from its cage to chase down the boat of fresh souls. The fin rose from the water, a steel sail of destruction. The guns rang out again and the creature disappeared, peppered with fresh wounds, leaking more blood and gore into the ocean.

"Let's move," the sergeant major spoke, pulling Marcus with him. The chopper was full, the motors whining.

Marcus followed, jumping up into the belly of the chopper. He took his place on the open ledge, refusing the offered seat in the middle of the soldiers.

"Here, I will let you have the honours," the sergeant major said as he handed the detonator over to Marcus. "There are two charges. We are going to lure her in with the first blast and take her apart with the second."

Marcus took the charge and gripped it tight. He was surprised to find his hands trembling. While he had been on the base, he had been able to immerse himself in the work. Now, with the detonator in his hand, the finality of everything, the emotions came at him with a rush. His redemption was at hand, and he was not yet ready.

Marcus looked at the sergeant major and nodded, and received the same in return. They did not need anything else. Between the two war horses, there were no words needed.

"On my signal, Agent."

"Yes, sir," Marcus answered.

***

The *Port Royal* remained ahead of the shark, keeping their distance, not letting the beast get close enough to launch an attack. The distance was managed through the guns.

"Sir, Omega-Base is clear," the radioman relayed the message from the helicopter.

"Dr. Lucas, if you would be so kind," Captain Hughes turned towards Martin.

"The chip is offline, I don't know who is doing this, but they are better than me at this computer shit. I'm banking on her still associating the base as being home." Martin turned away from the computer.

He was shocked to find that he was out of breath. He had been constantly working on the frequencies and pitches of the chip, working his way through the layers of biologic control. Much like picking a lock, accessing a mind without permission took skill, patience and time, and doing so while in competition with another living soul working against you was nigh impossible.

His task was done, with the chip lost, he could not do any more than he had. Martin had filled the shark's brain with images of the lab, and the base, all they had to do now was wait and hope for the best. Martin was exhausted. His battle had been fought on two fronts, against the creature, and against whoever was trying to stop him. He had won, but at a cost. His head ached.

"She is still coming, sir, she's five hundred feet behind us."

"Are you sure your plan worked, Doctor?" Hughes was starting to show the cracks in his character.

"Yes, we just need to give her a push in the right direction," Martin answered, faking his confidence.

"Four hundred yards, she is really motoring, coming at twenty-eight knots, sir."

"How do you mean the right direction, you were inside this creature's brain, right?" Hughes tried not to raise his voice as he spoke.

"Biometric control is not that simple. It is suggestion, subliminal messaging, or a sort. What I inserted is there, but her natural instincts are strong," Martin explained. "Besides, if the others have control over her, who knows what they are capable of."

"Three hundred yards, sir."

"You mean there is a chance they are driving that son of a bitch!" The captain tried hard to remain cool.

"I don't think so. I think they were just fighting my signal. I just don't understand how they knew about the chip at all. Unless..." Martin paused.

"Unless what, Dr. Lucas?" The captain pushed.

"Unless they had the shark this whole time. Maybe they are the ones that bred her, used the abandoned station against us." Martin shuddered at the thought.

"What would you suggest?" Hughes was looking at Martin. The fight was not his anymore. The enemy was not something he understood, and that realization did not sit comfortably with him.

"We need to get closer to Omega-Base-Six." Martin rose from behind his station and walked over to where the captain stood. "We circle around the base, once the shark is there we drop whatever torpedoes we can manage. Whether we score a direct hit of not, we turn and high-tail it out there." Martin's voice was a whisper. He was not sure why, but the words sounded better when spoken in soft tones.

"Two hundred yards, sir." The voice was pure panic.

"Change our course, we are going to loop around to the base. I want that 38 cannon smoking while we create some distance." The captain leaped to action, a second wind behind him.

The large ship turned sharply in the water, moving to cut back and pass around the far side of Omega-Base-Six. As they had expected, the shark duly followed. It rose above the water and was met with a barrage from the .98 calibre canon. The shots were fired fast and most went wide of the mark, but it was enough to drive the shark back down.

The base grew larger as the cruiser drew close. Martin stood in silence as he watched it grow. The poetry was there, and if anything he thought it a little too cliché, but so was life in the real world. The place where it started being the place where it ended. Not just for the shark, but for him also.

The base was evil. It had only ever seen to it that death and destruction came from within its imposing walls. From the death squad that had executed everybody on board, to the shark, the beast he had created. He had been responsible for taking the lives of more good, honest men and woman, a fact Martin for which Martin would never forgive himself.

***

Marcus watched as the cruiser made the turn around the condemned base and disappeared from view.

Marcus sat with the detonator in his hands, his scars tingled as he moved his eyes from the building, to the water, and to the detonator, and looping cycle of vision points. The end was close, and it made him smile.

"You okay there, Agent?" one of the younger men on the crew asked.

"I'm grand," Marcus answered with a smile.

The truth was, his palms were slick with sweat and his heart racing to the point where he was afraid it was just going to stop altogether.

"Just don't act until we get word from the front," the same young gun added.

The snide remark caught Marcus's attention. He turned to look at the man. "Fuck you, kid."

A silence fell over the chopper, the anger in the short, spat sentence was unmistakable. Marcus caught sight of the sergeant major sitting on the other side of the chopper. The grizzled veteran had a smile on his face.

The helicopter moved to circle around to get a better view of the show. Just as they moved into position, they saw it. The shark was flopping on the deck of the *Point Royal*, its large body thrashing and trashing the deck. It slid from the deck and back into the ocean, disappearing beneath the waves. Leaving behind it a boat that was rocking back and forth, its rear sinking down into the water.

***

"Sir, she's gone home," the technician called out.

"I want confirmation," Captain Hughes called out. He had one shot at it.

"Confirmed," the response came. "Wait," the correction followed immediately.

The shark leaped from the water beside them, coming up from under the boat on the far side of Omega-Base. It moved through the water like lightning and powered out of it like a locomotive. The whole body cleared the water and cleared the rear of the cruiser.

The ship lunged violently, as a booming crash rang out, shaking everybody in the command room down to their boots.

The entire ship was driven down into the water, the rear fully submerging. Men were swept from its deck and into the ocean. The creature thrashed and twisted its body. The jaws snapping shut around the Mk 38 cannon, the same one that inflicted so much pain on its body. Blood smeared the iron exterior of the craft as the shark powered its way over the deck, crashing through everything that stood in its path, before sliding back into the water.

By the time Captain Hughes had pulled himself to his feet, it was gone, as too was the vision in his left eye. Blood poured from his head and his ribs ached from where he had fallen against the console.

"Captain, we're taking on water," a voice cried out.

"The hull has been compromised," another called.

"Man overboard," a third voice rang out.

The warnings came thick and fast, and panic rang out around the command room.

"Engines, get us out of here." Captain Hughes ignored the warnings. They needed to move. "Tell the chopper to blow it, blow it now!" he roared, his voice a bellow of rage-driven authority. Blood flew from his lips as he coughed into his hand. His palm came away red with bloody spit.

***

Marcus heard the order, and without a second thought, pushed the detonator.

The first explosion happened underwater, and as such, the initial impact, the cacophonous detonation of the lower level was somewhat muted, but the result was clear. A ring of water rushed out from around the base. The water clouded and bubbled as if boiling. A few moments later, the second larger explosion ripped through the structure. What little integrity remained was removed in an expulsion that tore through iron, shattered glass and brought the entire structure collapsing in on itself. Fire leaped into the air and shot through the perforated exterior like dragon's breath.

A third round of detonations ripped through the central core of the structure, causing what remained to crumble. A thick black ball of smoke billowed into the air, riding on a rising pillar of flame.

The wall of water rose, and for a while, Omega-Base-Six was obscured. When it came back into view, the remains were a smouldering husk already nearly fully submerged.

A series of cheers broke out on the chopper which pulled up and away from the shock of the blast.

***

The *Port Royal* limped away from the base. Three of her turbine engines were damaged and one was lost completely.

She was too close to the base when the explosions rang out. The water seemed to bulge from the blast, swelling and rising but not bursting. The boat was pushed into the air, and when the blast finally erupted through the water, it was powerful enough to tip the *Port Royal* close to the edge of capsizing.

The shock wave of the blast hit the boat like a punch from some giant mech machine, only this impact was one everybody on the bridge managed to brace themselves for. The damaged rear was further submerged by the rising torrent, and while they managed to survive, the boat was more structurally impaired than anybody would have wanted.

If the shark had somehow survived, then it would be impossible for them to mount any form of resistance. Their weapons were gone, decimated by the body of the beast as it had squirmed its way over the deck.

"Captain," a voice called out.

"I'm alright, everybody else?" Captain Hughes wheezed and stared out of the hole in the front of the command room. The glass had been blown away by the blast. Shards littered the floor and blood flowed from the many wounds inflicted as the windows shattered.

"Did we get the bitch?" Hughes asked, looking around for anybody who would be in condition to give him a confirmation.

"I would say so, sir," a young seaman, who had been pulled onto the *Port Royal* in a bad case of being in the wrong place at the wrong time, answered, pointing out of the former window.

On the deck lay a large and bloodied dorsal fin. Thick strands of flesh and muscle dangled beneath the roughly torn-off appendage. The fin itself was torn open, the flesh bubbling up from within to explode out of the grey steel flesh.

A round of cheers went up, and for a moment, everybody forgot about the damaged vessel and the steadily rising water levels in the hull.

***

Boats were scrambled and the crew of the *Port Royal* were evacuated from the ship, and brought back to the shore.

The boat itself also limped back home with the help of two other vessels. It was brought back to Pearl Harbor where it was raised from the water, and at a much later date, officially retired.

Martin had never been happier to be on dry land. His entire body shook, not from the shock wave or from the repeated brushes with a potentially horrible and painful death, but because it was over. The beast he had created was dead, and so were a great many people. He held their deaths on his shoulders. His beast had turned and done this. His biometric devices had been used against him, against his country.

He stood on the dock and stared at the nearly disappeared shell of Omega-Base-Six. He tried to force it all out, let everything sink along with that place, but he didn't know how long it would last. There were some demons that would always find you again.

"So, we're done," Marcus said.

"Yes, I guess so," Martin answered, not breaking his seaward gaze.

"What are you going to do now?" Marcus asked, his own eyes also set firmly on the smoky horizon.

"I'm gonna sit down and have a drink. Not to get drunk, but because the last three days were the craziest motherfuckers of my life." Now Martin turned towards the man who had rapidly become his friend.

"Okay, but you're buying," Marcus said as he turned his back on the scene. He found it an easier task than he had expected.

"Me, you're the one who dragged me into this," Martin jokingly replied.

"Maybe, but I'm unemployed now, so I can't go buying comparative strangers drinks." Marcus smiled, the scars on his face creasing from the effort.

"They fired you?"

"I quit. I said goodbye out there, and I just don't feel it anymore. I'm not going back to being a paper pusher, and they won't put me back in the field because of all this." He drew an air circle around his mangled face.

"Alright, I'm buying, but only one. Then I was thinking about taking in one of those dancing shows. You know, the ones with the swivelling hips and grass skirts," Martin joked and the two friends walked away.

"Don't forget the coconut bras," Marcus added.

EPILOGUE

Martin stood on the beach, his toes digging into the sand. The sky above him was a glorious, cloudless shade of azure. The sand was white, glistening under the unshaded power for the sun. The sea was calm and as flat as a millpond. It would not be too long before the heat really rose, and the crowds came swarming in.

He would be long gone by then. He always was, but before that, before the day began and the families and locals flocked to the beach, their bodies bronzed and burned and every shade in between, Martin took his moment. He walked along the sand and then ran into the sea, diving deep below the surface, relishing the soul-quenching cool of the water as it embraced him.

He would swim until his arms grew tired, and then he would swim some more, not stopping until he had everything out of his system. He would collapse onto a towel by the shore, more often than not with tears in his eyes. He would lay back and think of the dead, those that had died as a result of his work.

He would never forget, and he try as he might, forgiveness was not an option, and so he did this. He followed his new ritual faithfully.

It had been eleven months since the incident in Hawaii, and ten months and twenty-eight days since he had turned down the offer he had been presented with.

Immeasurable funds, full control of all projects. It had been tempting, and the salary had been mind boggling. Yet Martin had walked away. He didn't need it anymore. He was empty, and all he wanted was a simple life.

A shadow fell over him on the beach.

"I thought I would find you here," the familiar voice spoke.

"I'm glad you found me," Martin answered, not bothering to open his eyes, as he lay drying in the sun.

Lynne dropped onto the towel beside him. She slowly traced a swirling pattern over his bare chest, before leaning in and planting a kiss on his cheek.

The time in Florida had done her good. The detox offered by the military had worked a treat. She had stopped dancing, taken up fitness as a better hobby to control the ghosts of her past and had lost close to twenty-five pounds.

She had not been expecting to see Martin again, having been told of his history, of his real identity. She was sad, but understood enough of how the world worked. She loved Martin, and because of that, she was willing to let him be himself again, once he got through the same detox program she had been in.

When he turned up on her doorstep one day, she had been shocked. They lived together in a beachside house far away from the big crowds and cities. Fully paid for by the government and with a bank balance that more than compensated Martin for everything he had done, they did not have a care in the world.

They lived life for the moment. They loved and laughed, and never fought.

Martin rolled over and pulled Lynne on top of him, kissing her deeply.

"Easy, tiger," she said with a smile. "We have company."

"Company?" Martin asked, as a sudden shiver ran over his body.

"Yes, back at the house. He said he is a friend of yours," Lynne spoke and Martin shot to his feet. The figure was standing on the front deck of the house, the sun catching his badly scarred face and making it shimmer like the surface of the ocean that bound their souls together.

"It's good to see you, Dr. Lucas," Marcus spoke, as grabbed his friend and hugged him tight.

"Likewise, buddy," Martin said, reciprocating the embrace.

"You two sit, I'll go and make some iced tea," Lynne said, smiling at the two. "You probably have a lot to talk about."

She left the two men sitting on the front porch, each man looking at the other, silence weighing heavily on them.

"You're looking good," Marcus said as he donned a pair of sunglasses.

"Thanks, you too."

Silence again.

"So, what have you been up to? Enjoying the retired life?" Marcus asked, looking around. "Quite the place you have here."

"Thanks, and yes, the quiet life suits me to the ground." Martin smiled. "What about you? Have you taken up golf with Director Cove?"

"Not exactly. It turned out Cove was one of them. He was involved in everything from a high level too. He used us to get control of the shark. They were hijacking your signal, bouncing it back to you." Marcus shifted, uncomfortable in the chair.

"So I was effectively fighting myself." Marin stared at his friend.

"Basically. So they got rid of Cove. Locked him up somewhere nice, damp and dark." Marcus took off his glasses, cleaned them and replaced them.

"You never know who you could trust. I pity the man who walks into that job. He will have people watching him like a fucking hawk," Martin said, settling back into his chair.

"I do," Marcus said with a smile.

"You!" Martin coughed. "I thought you were done with it all."

"I was, but that was before I knew." Marcus leaned forward.

"Knew what?" Lynne asked as she appeared carrying a tray with iced tea.

"Before I knew about the other beasts they created. I'm here because I wanted to check in on you. I'm here because I want to be, but I'm also here because I need your help, Dr. Lucas."

CHECK OUT OTHER GREAT
DEEP SEA THRILLERS

MEGA
by Jake Bible

There is something in the deep. Something large. Something hungry. Something prehistoric.
And Team Grendel must find it, fight it, and kill it.
Kinsey Thorne, the first female US Navy SEAL candidate has hit rock bottom. Having washed out of the Navy, she turned to every drink and drug she could get her hands on. Until her father and cousins, all ex-Navy SEALS themselves, offer her a way back into the life: as part of a private, elite combat Team being put together to find and hunt down an impossible monster in the Indian Ocean. Kinsey has a second chance, but can she live through it?

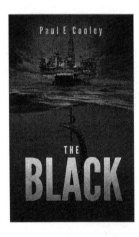

THE BLACK
by Paul E Cooley

Under 30,000 feet of water, the exploration rig Leaguer has discovered an oil field larger than Saudi Arabia, with oil so sweet and pure, nations would go to war for the rights to it. But as the team starts drilling exploration well after exploration well in their race to claim the sweet crude, a deep rumbling beneath the ocean floor shakes them all to their core. Something has been living in the oil and it's about to give birth to the greatest threat humanity has ever seen.

"The Black" is a techno/horror-thriller that puts the horror and action of movies such as Leviathan and The Thing right into readers' hands. Ocean exploration will never be the same."

SEVERED**PRESS**

CHECK OUT OTHER GREAT DEEP SEA THRILLERS

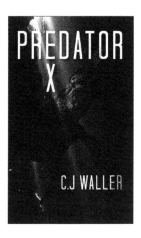

PREDATOR X
by C.J Waller

When deep level oil fracking uncovers a vast subterranean sea, a crack team of cavers and scientists are sent down to investigate. Upon their arrival, they disappear without a trace. A second team, including sedimentologist Dr Megan Stoker, are ordered to seek out Alpha Team and report back their findings. But Alpha team are nowhere to be found – instead, they are faced with something unexpected in the depths. Something ancient. Something huge. Something dangerous. Predator X

DEAD BAIT
by Tim Curran

A husband hell-bent on revenge hunts a Wereshark...A Russian mail order bride with a fishy secret...Crabs with a collective consciousness...A vampire who transforms into a Candiru...Zombie piranha...Bait that will have you crawling out of your skin and more. Drawing on horror, humor with a helping of dark fantasy and a touch of deviance, these 19 contemporary stories pay homage to the monsters that lurk in the murky waters of our imaginations. If you thought it was safe to go back in the water...Think Again!

CHECK OUT OTHER GREAT
DEEP SEA THRILLERS

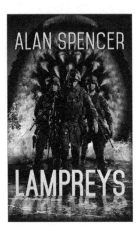

LAMPREYS
by Alan Spencer

A secret government tactical team is sent to perform a clean sweep of a private research installation. Horrible atrocities lurk within the abandoned corridors. Mutated sea creatures with insane killing abilities are waiting to suck the blood and meat from their prey.

Unemployed college professor Conrad Garfield is forced to assist and is soon separated from the team. Alone and afraid, Conrad must use his wits to battle mutated lampreys, infected scientists and go head-to-head with the biggest monstrosity of all.

Can Conrad survive, or will the deadly monsters suck the very life from his body?

DEEP DEVOTION
by M.C. Norris

Rising from the depths, a mind-bending monster unleashes a wave of terror across the American heartland. Kate Browning, a Kansas City EMT confronts her paralyzing fear of water when she traces the source of a deadly parasitic affliction to the Gulf of Mexico. Cooperating with a marine biologist, she travels to Florida in an effort to save the life of one very special patient, but the source of the epidemic happens to be the nest of a terrifying monster, one that last rose from the depths to annihilate the lost continent of Atlantis.

Leviathan, destroyer, devoted lifemate and parent, the abomination is not going to take the extermination of its brood well.

 SEVEREDPRESS

CHECK OUT OTHER GREAT
DEEP SEA THRILLERS

THEY RISE
by Hunter Shea

Some call them ghost sharks, the oldest and strangest looking creatures in the sea.

Marine biologist Brad Whitley has studied chimaera fish all his life. He thought he knew everything about them. He was wrong. Warming ocean temperatures free legions of prehistoric chimaera fish from their methane ice suspended animation. Now, in a corner of the Bermuda Triangle, the ocean waters run red. The 400 million year old massive killing machines know no mercy, destroying everything in their path. It will take Whitley, his climatologist ex-wife and the entire US Navy to stop them in the bloodiest battle ever seen on the high seas.

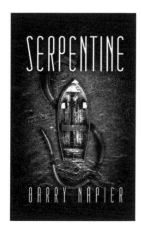

SERPENTINE
by Barry Napier

Clarkton Lake is a picturesque vacation spot located in rural Virginia, great for fishing, skiing, and wasting summer days away.

But this summer, something is different. When butchered bodies are discovered in the water and along the muddy banks of Clarkton Lake, what starts out as a typical summer on the lake quickly turns into a nightmare.

This summer, something new lives in the lake...something that was born in the darkest depths of the ocean and accidentally brought to these typically peaceful waters.

It's getting bigger, it's getting smarter...and it's always hungry.

CHECK OUT OTHER GREAT
DEEP SEA THRILLERS

SEA RAPTOR
by John J. Rust

From terrorist hunter to monster hunter! Jack Rastun was a decorated U.S. Army Ranger, until an unfortunate incident forced him out of the service. He is soon hired by the Foundation for Undocumented Biological Investigation and given a new mission, to search for cryptids, creatures whose existence has not been proven by mainstream science. Teaming up with the daring and beautiful wildlife photographer Karen Thatcher, they must stop a sea monster's deadly rampage along the Jersey Shore. But that's not the only danger Rastun faces. A group of murderous animal smugglers also want the creature. Rastun must utilize every skill learned from years of fighting, otherwise, his first mission for the FUBI might very well be his last.

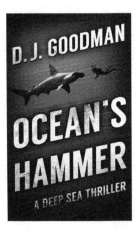

OCEAN'S HAMMER
by D.J. Goodman

Something strange is happening in the Sea of Cortez. Whales are beaching for no apparent reason and the local hammerhead shark population, previously believed to be fished to extinction, has suddenly reappeared. Marine biologists Maria Quintero and Kevin Hoyt have come to investigate with a television producer in tow, hoping to get footage that will land them a reality TV show. The plan is to have a stand-off against a notorious illegal shark-fishing captain and then go home.

Things are not going according to plan.

There is something new in the waters of the Sea of Cortez. Something smart. Something huge. Something that has its own plans for Quintero and Hoyt.

CHECK OUT OTHER GREAT
DEEP SEA THRILLERS

MEGATOOTH
by Viktor Zarkov

When the death rate of sperm whales rises dramatically, a well-respected environmental activist puts together a ragtag team to hit the high seas to investigate the matter. They suspect that the deaths are due to poachers and they are all driven by a need for justice.

Elsewhere, an experimental government vessel is enhancing deep sea mining equipment. They see one of these dead whales up close and personal...and are fairly certain that it wasn't poachers that killed it.

Both of these teams are about to discover that poachers are the least of their worries. There is something hunting the whales...

Something big
Something prehistoric.
Something terrifying.
MEGATOOTH!

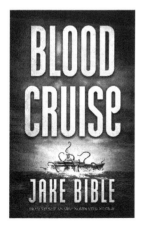

BLOOD CRUISE
by Jake Bible

Ben Clow's plans are set. Drop off kids, pick up girlfriend, head to the marina, and hop on best friend's cruiser for a weekend of fun at sea. But Ben's happy plans are about to be changed by a tentacled horror that lurks beneath the waves.

International crime lords! Deep cover black ops agents! A ravenous, bloodsucking monster! A storm of evil and danger conspire to turn Ben Clow's vacation from a fun ocean getaway into a nightmare of a Blood Cruise!

Made in the USA
Middletown, DE
25 November 2016